PENGUIN
SPECIALS

Penguin Specials fill a gap. Written by some of today's most exciting and insightful writers, they are short enough to be read in a single sitting — when you're stuck on a train; in your lunch hour; between dinner and bedtime. Specials can provide a thought-provoking opinion, a primer to bring you up to date, or a striking piece of fiction. They are concise, original and affordable.

To browse digital and print Penguin Specials titles, please refer to **www.penguin.com.au/penguinspecials**

The Debt Collector

by

WANG SHOU

Translated from the
original Chinese

By John Frederick Franz

PENGUIN BOOKS

UK | USA | Canada | Ireland | Australia
India | New Zealand | South Africa | China

Penguin Books is part of the Penguin Random House group of companies
whose addresses can be found at global.penguinrandomhouse.com

Penguin
Random House
PENGUIN BOOKS

This paperback edition published by Penguin Group (Australia), 2019

1 3 5 7 9 10 8 6 4 2

Text copyright © Wang Shou, 2019

Translated from the Chinese by John Frederick Franz

Produced with Writers Association of Zhejiang Province

Originally published in Chinese as *Futou duole ziji de bing*
with the Writers Association of Zhejiang Province

The moral right of the author has been asserted.

Cover design by Di Suo © Penguin Group (Australia)
Text design by Steffan Leyshon-Jones © Penguin Group (Australia)
Printed and bound in China by RR Donnelley Asia Printing Solutions Ltd.

ISBN: 9780734398703

penguin.com.au

About the Translator

Born and raised in New Rochelle, NY, Fred Franz became interested in things Chinese at an early age and has lived and worked in both China and Japan on many different occasions over the past 35 years. He now divides his time between Southeast Asia, the Colorado Rockies and the coast of Spain.

Getting Zhang Guoliang to Leave Jiangxi

After long deliberation, Chen Sheng decided to go to Jiangxi and get Zhang Guoliang to come back with him.

Chen Sheng sold glue and moulded plastic stripping at the market. These were the two things needed for the manufacture of shoes; one to glue them together and the other to make liners. Chen Sheng was mostly satisfied with his business. He had originally been in the army, though he had never seen action nor picked up a gun. He had served instead in military logistics, raising pigs for the mess hall. When he was discharged, his commanding officer gave him two choices, first, he could arrange a job for him, or second, he could receive a small pension. Chen Sheng chose the latter. After returning home, he borrowed some money from friends and started his business.

Doing business in Rezhou had never been all that difficult, but Chen Sheng had one problem – he extended credit too easily. He extended credit to buyers who had no money, as well to those who had, and it was this lack of discipline that inevitably made it difficult for him to succeed. Chen Sheng had been in business for ten years by then. Sometimes he had to hustle when business was slow and would barely make enough to eat. At other times, business was not too bad. Eventually, he had become accustomed to both.

The Feida Shoe Company had always bought the glue and moulded plastic strips they needed to make their shoes from Chen Sheng. They always settled their debts quickly at the start, so their business relationship progressively expanded. Later on, maybe because of a bad economy, maybe due to a season of lousy sales, maybe because of bad marketing, or maybe even because the shoes they made were of poor quality – the debt the boss of Feida owed eventually reached 300 000 *yuan*, and this was when he decided to renege on it. Chen Sheng knew the debt was not due to any of the aforementioned reasons, but was really because the Feida boss was devoid of any conscience.

Chen Sheng thought of many different ways to try and settle the matter. He tried getting a friend to mediate, then even specially invited the Feida boss out for dinner, prepared to offer him a one-time discount on the debt. He really didn't mind taking a loss on the debt, he just didn't want it staying stuck in his craw. However, the Feida boss wouldn't yield at all. Even his tone of voice was hard as steel when telling Chen Sheng that if it was money he wanted, he wouldn't get any, but if he wanted shoes instead, then he had piles and he could come and take some if he wanted.

Chen Sheng asked him, 'What are you on about? You can't hold me responsible for seasonal downturns, lousy economic conditions, or your own lousy marketing!'

The boss retorted, 'Well then, what if I were to tell everyone that it was your materials that'd ruined my shoes! How'd you like that?'

Chen Sheng replied, 'Even if it had been my materials that ruined your shoes, this is surely not the time to tell me!' The boss remarked, 'I only just found out that this was the reason. That's why I'm telling you now! Not only am I not asking you to make good on your lousy materials, but I'm also offering to pay you in kind! I'm being just about as polite as I know how to be!'

This was not what Chen Sheng wanted to hear, but he could tell from the hardness of the Feida boss' speech that this situation would not be easily resolved.

Some of the men who ran businesses in Rezhou had a mysterious air about them. They all originally had connections with the underworld, carried machetes in their belts and swaggered when they walked. Having now grown older and wanting to put their roguishness behind them, they had established small factories as a means of supporting themselves. In reality, however, their business practices remained just as sketchy as ever. They were shysters and connivers to the core. The Feida boss was one of them.

Chen Sheng, of course, was not to be trifled with either. After all, he had been in the army, so he clearly had some guts. He also knew that with a matter such as this, he would have to outsmart the Feida boss, not attack him head-on. He would have to employ a different strategy, perhaps like one he had once seen in a movie, if he was going to break through this stalemate and get his money back. This was why he thought of Zhang Guoliang.

When Chen Sheng first went into business, he not only sold his products but also did some work on the side for other factories processing the plastic strips and fitting them to shoes. Zhang Guoliang had worked for him at that time processing the scraps. The good thing about him was that he was especially able, especially tough, and except for when eating or relieving himself, he was always right on the money in whatever he was doing.

One day, Chen Sheng discovered five plastic sheets had gone missing from the factory. *Who could have taken them?* There were only a few people who went in and out of the factory; there was Chen Sheng, then there was the manager, the shipper, and Zhang Guoliang, who processed the scraps. Chen Sheng told them, 'I'll give you all a day to think about it. It would be best if those sheets were to make their way back to where they originally were. If they do, then I'll let bygones be bygones and pretend the theft never happened.'

However, no one ever let on that they knew a thing. Everyone acted innocently and naturally nothing was ever returned. Chen Sheng could not afford for them not to take him seriously since it would damage his position as the boss, so he instead chose to report it to the authorities.

When Chen Sheng arrived at the police station, the cop there told him, 'This will be easy. Bring 'em down here and I'll scare the crap out of 'em !'

Chen Sheng told him, 'Please, don't beat them! What if it isn't them? I'll still need them to work for me!'

The cop asked him, 'Then whaddya want me to do, invite 'em out on a dinner date?'

Chen Sheng exclaimed, 'It's not like they're my slaves! If you beat them, they may resent me forever. Maybe you can just yell at them a little.'

The cop told him, 'You're too soft, and the next time you're out of luck, it's going to be your own fault.'

Chen Sheng merely smiled sheepishly.

When the cop arrived at Chen Sheng's factory, he called everyone related to the case together and lined them up. It was like something out of a movie, the way he paced back and forth in front of them, staring first at their feet, then keenly at their eyes. The cop circled them, staring even more attentively at them in line from behind. After only a minute or so, Zhang Guoliang began fidgeting, shuffling his hands around from his back to his front. When the cop had returned to face them, he could see that of the three people there, only Zhang Guoliang's face had turned white. Poking Zhang Guoliang in the chest, he told him dramatically, 'You! Come with me!'

After the policeman led away Zhang Guoliang, there were a few things that Chen Sheng couldn't get out of his mind. *What if it wasn't him and the cop still beat him? What if he had nobody left to work for him, and what if Zhang Guoliang had it in for him after the interrogation?* He couldn't stand it any longer, so around noon, Chen Sheng went down to the police station to stealthily have a look at what might be going on there. From a distance, Chen Sheng spied Zhang Guoliang standing by some stairs. It looked as if the policeman was punishing him by forcing him to stand motionless in a martial arts position used in Qigong; a position where one facilitates an out-of-body experience by standing perfectly still. When he looked even more closely, however, he could see that Zhang Guoliang's hand was shackled to the railing of the staircase while he stood awkwardly on one leg, supporting all his body weight on just a few toes. This was clearly a crafty method the cop was using to torture him, for it wouldn't leave any marks that would indicate that he'd been beaten. Still, it was still a kind of torture nonetheless.

Chen Sheng thought, *If this keeps up, Zhang Guoliang is likely to hate me. What if I come home one day and find my windows smashed by rocks or my gutters plugged up with straw? What then?*

That afternoon and evening, Chen Sheng sent over twenty meat dumplings to Zhang Guoliang, ten for each meal. He thought he might send some other food and drink over as well, but when he considered how Zhang Guoliang couldn't really move at all, he gave up on the idea. Finally, about twenty-four hours later, the police released Zhang Guoliang, freeing him to return home. The cop told him, 'It wasn't him.'

Relieved, Chen Sheng replied, 'I'm glad it's not him.'

The cop asked him, 'Do you want me to bring the others in for questioning?'

Chen Sheng said hastily, 'Forget about it.'

The cop told him that Zhang Guoliang had indeed never confessed to any details, and this is why he had released him.

Chen Sheng then asked, 'Then, why was it only his face that turned white?'

The cop told him that some people were just like that, they become terrified in the presence of cops and get nervous for no reason at all. Some inexplicably become apprehensive whenever a thing like this happens. Even if a crime has nothing to do with them, they begin feeling guilty. In psychiatry, they call it an obsessive-compulsive disorder. It's like they start feeling sick when they're really not.

The cop touched on one other particular detail that he had deduced from his interrogation. Zhang Guoliang told him he had a wet dream the night before. A nocturnal emission will usually only occur during very deep sleep, or when a person has very strange dreams. Had Zhang Guoliang really been guilty, he would probably have laid awake all night which would have precluded him from having any kind of a wet dream, so the theft could not have had anything to do with him.

Later that day, Chen Sheng gave Zhang Guoliang another fifty *yuan*, telling him that it was for overtime, and for emotional compensation as well. Zhang Guoliang hesitated at first, but then took it. Chen Sheng reckoned Zhang Guoliang would most likely pack up his things and clear out the next day. After all, he had been injured without cause, and there was sure to be much he'd be dissatisfied about. However, Zhang Guoliang never said anything about it at all and chose to keep on working there as if nothing had ever happened.

Zhang Guoliang had returned to his hometown the previous winter, saying he had wanted to renovate his house during the spring, and to tend to a few rows of mushrooms in the summer. Chen Sheng understood the thinking of people from the countryside and why Zhang Guoliang could not remain in the city of Rezhou for very long. He was older now, his family needed him, and there were many things he could not attend to if he continued to stay and work in city. Now, Chen Sheng found himself aboard a train riding south. He had no idea what Zhang Guoliang's situation at home was like, but he needed to bring him back with him to Rezhou. He needed his help with something. He needed some-one, someone reliable like Zhang Guoliang.

Since Chen Sheng had never been to Zhang Guoliang's home before, he had no idea what to expect. During past Spring Festivals, Chen Sheng had always wanted his workers to return to Rezhou as soon as they could to start working again. Chen Sheng would call each of them one by one, urging them to put aside their family affairs and, like a flock of birds, fly back to Rezhou as quick as they could. This time, however, Chen Sheng made no phone calls. He felt the thing this time was just too big, and that it was not something he could easily discuss over the phone. There was just no way to do it justice over the phone. He had no choice but to go himself to Zhang Guoliang's home, to go in person and stand right in front of him. He had to do this if he were to ever make Zhang Guoliang understand that this thing he needed help with was no trivial matter. That way he could not just dismiss it out of hand.

Zhang Guoliang's hometown was in Jiangxi Province, in Le'an County, a small village in Le'an, called Jiang'an to be precise. This flimsy clue was all that Chen Sheng had to go on when it came to locating Zhang Guoliang. All he knew before about Jiangxi was that the story 'Starting a Revolution with Two Kitchen Knives' had come from there. He had found that story at the time to be a bit comical, that perhaps it might not have been the most brilliant image to convey revolutionary ideals. Could their poverty have been so dire if they still had two kitchen knives? *Most households these days have only one knife. How could they have possibly had two back then?* Later, when a great influx of labourers began pouring into Rezhou, most of them had come in from Jiangxi. That was when Chen Sheng began realising that compared with villagers from other inland provinces like Anhui, Hunan, Guizhou and so on, the villagers from Jiangxi were just a little more reserved. This was yet another reason why Chen Sheng felt it might be a surer thing if he were to go himself to personally call on Zhang Guoliang at his home.

Chen Sheng had done some homework before setting out, so he knew the general direction of Le'an. Le'an was situated in the northern part of Jiangxi, and by looking at the colours on the map, he could tell it was quite a mountainous area. There were no direct routes there, and the quality of the roads once he got there wouldn't be much to speak of either.

However, one special geographical landmark stood out on the map, and that was the station of the 261st National Geographical Team. This gave Chen Sheng faith that, by first taking the train to Nanchang, he could afterwards transfer to a local cargo truck heading in the right direction. The reason cargo trucks would be running in that direction was because of a uranium mine located there. It was a uranium mine, yet it had never really brought any kind of prosperity to the area. It had been quietly operating for many years by then, but had never really helped the local economy. Any other kind of mine, even a coal or a rock mine, would from the beginning have been a much greater boon to the local economy. A uranium mine was useless to people's livelihoods. It was useless to local development, and uranium itself has always had a bad reputation. Truckload after truckload of uranium ore was being sent out of there, but no one really knew where it went off to be refined or where it was ultimately used. There was an awful lot of mystery that surrounded the whole affair.

The long journey Chen Sheng was making now was also very mysterious. Whether his plan succeeded or failed, he had determined that he would keep the whole thing a secret. He could not afford even the slightest of slip-ups. Outside the window of the train lay an unbroken range of hills with houses scattered here and there among them. There were rectangular fields of rapeseed and flooded rice paddies reflecting the light. There were black cows, standing alone against the landscape, and elderly country bumpkins watching from the sidelines as the train passed by. Men and women, in groups of three or four, were transplanting rice seedlings in the paddies, and children with rice bowls in their hands giggled foolishly upon the paddy banks. There were flowering peach trees, and occasionally pear trees. The sky would grow dark, and then light again. It would rain for a while, and then clear up again.

He ate when hungry and napped when tired, and when the train arrived, he then transferred to a cargo truck. He rode until the mountain road ended, then walked until it gradually became no more than a footpath between the paddies. Actually, Chen Sheng had already arrived in Jiang'an village by afternoon. Perhaps because that village was never visited by outsiders, or perhaps because it was backwards and poor, but Chen Sheng felt as if the people he met on the road were scrutinising everything about him. He felt their greedy and doubtful stares. It made him feel as if he were the least bit careless that they might try to even devour him whole. Yet, Chen Sheng somehow found ways to kill time until nightfall before he gradually approached

Zhang Guoliang's house. He had already asked around as to the whereabouts of Zhang Guoliang's mushroom shed, and was just then standing outside it, waiting, when suddenly Zhang Guoliang came dashing out from the shed, almost running into and startling Chen Sheng. Zhang Guoliang gaped at Chen Sheng in astonishment, then queried, 'Boss, how did you get here? It's like you just floated down from out of the sky!'

Chen Sheng murmured, 'I am a little woozy myself!'

That evening, Chen Sheng and Zhang Guoliang spoke of many things inside his dusky little house. Zhang Guoliang spoke of his plans to renovate his house, of his chances for marriage and how slim they were, and then went on at length about the various difficulties involved in farming. However, what they mostly spoke about was the 300 000 *yuan* debt owed to Chen Sheng, and the plan Chen Sheng wanted them to undertake together, a plan to get his money back pronto. Chen Sheng told him how they would do it, why it was feasible, and what they would need to carry it out.

Of course, they also talked about how they would split the profit. Chen Sheng told Zhang Guoliang that if they were successful, he would give him 10 per cent of that original amount owed to him. And if they were not successful? If Zhang Guoliang were caught, or if he ended up in jail, in a worst-case scenario like that, Chen Sheng agreed to give him 30 000 *yuan* in compensation every year he was locked up. If Zhang Guoliang were locked-up in Rezhou, he would be making shoes, or if he was sent off to Jinzhou, he'd be making bricks. If he got out in say, three to five years, he would then have more than 100 000 yuan waiting for him. It would be easy money!

During the whole time they'd talked, what kept flashing inside Zhang Guoliang's brain was how Chen Sheng had treated him back when he was his boss. He felt his old boss was alright, he felt that he could trust him. When he added this to the fact that he was poor and needed money, he didn't oppose the plan in principle and thought that he might want to give it a try. After all, the greater the risk, the greater the reward, the greater the difficulty involved, the more especially exciting success seemed. Both of them had faced challenges before, and both understood that sometimes, in order to win, one had to be willing to put everything on the line. Zhang Guoliang found that if he looked at it primarily as a business trip, he could immediately warm-up to the idea. Toward the end of their conversation, Chen Sheng told him, 'Don't worry about a thing. Since this is my idea, I'll make sure you're taken care of and when we're done that you get home in one piece.'

Staking Out the Housing Complex for Two Days

It was four days later when Chen Sheng arrived with Zhang Guoliang at the front gate of the Carnival housing complex. He told Zhang Guoliang that the boss who owed him money lived in Building 3 in Block A. Chen Sheng then led Zhang Guoliang across the street to a house sitting kitty-corner to the housing complex. There was a public park in its final stages of construction, so the noise and activity of the building works made it the perfect place for a couple of strangers to prowl about unnoticed. The house had originally been a well-to-do farmer's residence, and when the area had officially been designated for construction of a public park, the house had originally been slated for demolition as well, but by some fluke it had been preserved, and had now become the construction office for all the demolition and renovation work. Now that the road had been paved and the construction of the park was nearly complete, the house's mission was near completion as well. It was planned to be turned into a small teahouse by the entrance to the park or be demolished with a new service facility or something similar built in its place. Chen Sheng was presently using it as an observation tower, a place to watch the comings and goings of others.

He had known of this spot early on, but had never really made any effort to get it prepared for what he had been planning to do. Even three days earlier, when he had just arrived back to Rezhou with Zhang Guoliang, he was still hesitant about his plan. He had hoped he wouldn't have to carry out his plan frantically, for it might cause him to become careless, or to become negligent. He hoped to be settled down, so he could gradually digest the plan's procedure, so the plan would be thorough and dependable. The same went for Zhang Guoliang, Chen Sheng wanted him able to carefully determine what his objectives were, to be able to weigh out the plan's pros and cons clearly.

Over the next three days, Chen Sheng feted Zhang Guoliang with lots of delicious food and plenty of booze. This was over and above the monetary compensation he had already promised Zhang Guoliang, for all he really wanted now was to keep him satisfied for the next few days so he wouldn't begin getting cold feet, or start thinking about backing out of the plan.

For three days, Chen Sheng deliberately remained together with Zhang Guoliang, eating and drinking. They were holed up in a private inn that didn't require their real names to register. The staff at private inns were more casual as well, their management a little more lax. The pair never set foot outside their room, fearing someone might notice and begin gossiping about them. They ate, drank and relieved themselves all inside the room. They spread the delicacies they'd brought with them sumptuously out on the table, living it up, drinking late into each night together before ultimately passing out. However, Chen Sheng never really slept deeply, keeping one eye open, thinking he might perhaps determine something of Zhang Guoliang's true intentions while he slept. Sometimes people talked in their sleep and inadvertently revealed clues about their true emotions. *Would he talk in his sleep? Would he awaken suddenly from a nightmare?*

In any case, perhaps the beds at the inn were too comfortable, or perhaps they had drunk too much alcohol, but Zhang Guoliang always slept like a dead pig. He never tossed nor turned in the slightest, to the point where sometimes it seemed as if he even stopped breathing. Twice, he slept right through the night until the dawn, and once he got up in the middle of the night to relieve himself, then went right back to sleep again. Chen Sheng took this to be an indication of how extremely determined Zhang Guoliang was, and this served to finally bring him a little peace of mind.

Chen Sheng and Zhang Guoliang wanted to get inside the house, but the front door had already been locked, so they climbed in through a window toward the rear of the building. Downstairs, the house was filled with discarded tables and chairs belonging to the previous occupants, and the second floor was the same. Both these floors were useless to them, so they ascended directly to the third. Chen Sheng had already put in a few simple things on the third floor like a case of bottled water as well as a case of biscuits. He had wiped clean an old couch there, and had even placed a cotton quilt over it. He had also leaned some wooden boards against an outside window in such a way that they could conceal themselves, yet look outside and have six different lines of sight at the same time. This essentially turned the place into a watchtower.

Now, as Chen Sheng and Zhang Guoliang holed up inside that small room stocked with supplies, it gave them an illusion of safety. They were able to recklessly spy on people outside without them ever being aware of their two sets of prying eyes that were hiding inside. Of course, they were not there to watch the hustle and bustle of the goings on outside, nor to watch the cars with their lights twinkling like stars passing by, nor the unhurried pedestrians languidly walking the streets beneath them. They were there to surveil a villa in the Carnival housing complex opposite and familiarise themselves with, hopefully even come to know well, the people who were living there. This was the Feida boss, Long Haisheng, as well as his family.

It was a Saturday over a two-day holiday and from six in the morning, the parking spaces along the street below were gradually beginning to fill up. The park had still not been completely finished, they were still putting the finishing touches on the entrance area, as well as on the outer walls, but the interior of the park had essentially been completed. By this time, those who enjoyed exercising in the morning already couldn't wait to get in. A morning exercise called 'power-walking' had recently become popular with different people. You could often see them walking one behind the other along the street, but how could the city streets possibly compare with the park? There were small hills in the park and streams as well. The small paths inside the park were smooth and winding, far more interesting than the city streets, and there were lots of them as well. People were already waiting anxiously to get in, for they had early on mapped out the park and the routes they were going to use when they finally got to move their power-walking exercise inside.

Chen Sheng taught Zhang Guoliang how to spy from the window, how to filter, focus, and accurately find his objective amongst the chaos below. The Carnival complex was situated diagonally, right in front of them. You could say no one else was more familiar with the Carnival complex than Chen Sheng was, since he had already been there countless times trying to collect on his debt. The C Block was the first row of short buildings near the front gate. These screened off the inner neighbourhoods and made the complex seem even more mysterious and exotic inside. B Block was a semi-circle of attached townhomes that created another kind of screen separating it from the other residential neighbourhoods. A Block, the most luxurious of the neighbourhoods, consisted of five sets of finely constructed townhomes situated around a central plaza that included a garden and a fishpond. Chen Sheng told Zhang Guoliang that Long Haisheng lived in Building 3 in A Block, that if you went in and turned to your right, that it would be the building just by the side of the road.

The housing complex had been luxurious from the start, but now that a new park had been constructed across the street, the owners of its townhomes would surely want to go out to check out its marvelous new surroundings. Even if they had never had any interest in exercise before, Chen Sheng felt that, once they entered the park, they would be bitten by the power-walking bug. With this in mind, Chen Sheng believed Long Haisheng's family would certainly be interested in going to have a look at the park too, for even if they wouldn't go to exercise, they would at least want to see what all the hubbub was about. He was certain that they would at least go out for a stroll over that two-day holiday, and he wanted to introduce them one by one to Zhang Guoliang so that he would recognise them the next time he saw them.

People were sporadically coming out of the housing project and going in as well. Everyone going in was stopped at the gate and examined by security guards as befitted a high-end housing complex. Those bringing in take-out food, the interior decorators and renovators, and those collecting the garbage all kept a low profile. You could tell who they were just by looking at them, for they carried none of the arrogant air that the homeowners had. Just then, a group of people began nonchalantly walking out of the complex. Chen Sheng exclaimed, 'Look! It's them!'

Zhang Guoliang snapped to attention and immediately began to feel the blood rise inside of him.

As the two of them stared intensely ahead, Chen Sheng pointed out each member of the family to him one by one, almost like a tour guide. 'The one in front, the man wearing the loose-fitting clothes, that's Long Haisheng. Don't be fooled by his appearance, by the fact that he looks like a piano teacher. He's nothing like that in real life. The woman beside him wearing the green and white tracksuit is his wife. She's a full-time housewife. Do you know what a full-time housewife does? She just lazes around the house doing nothing all day. The child, and the woman who looks like she's from the countryside, walking five or six meters behind them, are his daughter and her nanny.'

Chen Sheng asked him, 'Do you see the nanny? Do you see the picnic basket in her hand? Did you ever see anyone with a picnic basket like that out in the countryside where you're from? No, probably not. You will only see them here in the city. You will only see rich people like these in the city as well. Inside that basket are tiered bento boxes full of things to eat, things like milk, cakes, eggs, fruits and whatnot. They live like kings! They're just pretending they're going out to exercise now. Look at the big deal they make about stretching out their backs and loosening their legs. Do you really believe they're going to exercise? They lay about their house all day, and all they're doing is just going out for some fresh air. In a minute they'll be sitting in some cool pavilion, snacking on the food they brought to eat while taking in the scenery.'

Chen Sheng was clearly trying to get Zhang Guoliang worked up. 'Have you ever lived like that?'

Zhang Guoliang shook his head. Chen Sheng then told him, 'Even I don't live like that, so I know you couldn't possibly either.'

Chen Sheng's talk began irritating Zhang Guoliang, and he began feeling a little bit of hatred for the rich rising up inside him.

Chen Sheng again asked Zhang Guoliang, 'Do you see how Long Haisheng walks? See how his right leg is unsteady, how it really seems to hurt, how he limps on his toes, then quickly takes the weight off of that leg?'

Zhang Guoliang looked carefully, then tentatively nodded his head.

Chen Sheng asked him, 'The reason I'm telling you this is so you will know that he only has one good leg. He has no strength in his other leg, so if you ever had to fight him, you needn't be afraid. He is nothing but a paper tiger.'

Zhang Guoliang asked him, 'How do you know so much about him?'

Chen Sheng answered, 'I used to know him before, when he had an operation. While young, he injured his back in a fight and that injury gradually began influencing his gait as he got older. He was in pain day and night, had to lie down a lot and not get up much. It made it hard for him even to do business, so he finally had no choice but to have an operation. Do you know what his disease is called? It's called trauma-induced narrowing of the spinal cord. He just had some swelling at first, but it gradually built up and calcified, putting pressure on and killing his nerves to the point where he couldn't even walk anymore.'

Zhang Guoliang told him, 'I know what you mean. A person's back is like the neck of a duck, like the ones that we have in the countryside. It's all nerves. You can paralyse a duck just by gently twisting its neck.'

Chen Sheng asked, 'Do you know how I knew him back then? It was because of our business relationship that we used to socialise with one another. The thing is, people like him are hard-hearted and will forget about you after the fact. You can forget about human kindness with them, since they really don't have any principles. There's really nothing much else you can do with them but force them into doing what we are doing. We really have no other choice at this point.'

At this point, Zhang Guoliang asked a silly question, 'Boss, if you are so familiar with the situation and have such good insider information, then why don't you just do this yourself? Why do you need me?'

Chen Sheng looked at him, then sighed deeply, thinking, This is the same old Zhang Guoliang, no different than the one I knew before. It seems clear that I will need to explain some things to him, otherwise he will never be able to pull this thing off and might end up really screwing things up.

Chen Sheng paused for a moment then said, 'First get it through your head that we're not going to kill anybody! Would I have brought you here if I wanted to kill him? If I had wanted to kill him, I would have done it by now, and why even do it unless I didn't want to keep on living myself, right? The reason we are here is to collect on a debt. I just want to frighten him a little in order to get my money back. Now I'll answer your silly question. He knows me. We still do business together. How could I openly force him to do something like this? Whether I succeeded or not, it would destroy my reputation. How could I ever remain in Rezhou? How could I ever remain in the circles I am in now? You, on the other hand, have no relationship with him at all. He doesn't even know you. You just need to go in there and scare him a little. Even if we don't succeed, I can always manage to hustle you back home to Jiangxi. Why do you think we've never gone out on the street since you've been here? Why do you think I've kept you locked up so tight? Isn't it so that no one will ever know you've been to Rezhou? It will be like you were never here, like you had been some kind of superhero.' Chen Sheng told him, 'We are ultimately here for the same reason. What we're doing now is making sure our plan is surefire, making sure it stays top-secret, then no one will ever have any inkling of what we've been up to.' Zhang Guoliang listened, nodding his head intently.

Chen Sheng went on to tell Zhang Guoliang that the fundamental condition that would ensure their success was the fact that Long Haisheng wanted to go on living, for he loved his life now. If Long Haisheng were still a hoodlum, or still involved with the underworld, if he didn't have such a big home and big business, then there wouldn't be any point in doing what they were doing. If he didn't have so much to lose, then he would have been far more ruthless and determined than they could ever have hoped to have been. 'You saw his situation today. He has a wonderful family. In a minute when they go to the park, he will start exercising by walking backwards. He's trying to watch his health. His wife is much younger than he is. He used his money and his power in order to get her, so he treasures her. He is even older than I am, in his fifties, with a very young child, not past the first or second grade, and it's not so easy to have a child so late in life. They've even employed a full-time nanny, so you could say they lead pretty terrific lives. Most people like him would easily part with their money if it meant saving their lives. They'll spend their money to avoid a calamity, and this will give us our opportunity. This is why we need to have confidence in our plan. Moreover, he knows very well in his heart that he owes money to too many people, that if someone has come to find him, then there must be a reason for it. He'd only need a minute to think before he really got the picture. He already lives with a guilty conscience, expecting that someday, someone is bound to show up at his door demanding to make good on some debt.'

That day, Chen Sheng and Zhang Guoliang talked about these things up on the third floor of the house while standing by the window peeking outside under the cover of the wooden planks. It was very noisy outside, it was bustling with activity. The people on the streets had mostly come to shop, but even more had come just to relax in the park. They could see everyone outside quite clearly without anyone having any inkling they were there, and this Chen Sheng and Zhang Guoliang found very amusing.

Tired of standing, they sat down for a bit on the couch, and even lay down a little. There was water for when they were thirsty and snacks for when they got hungry. Relieving themselves wasn't a problem either, for outside the window in the back of the building, was an unkempt hillside. By standing on a chair, they could aim themselves out the window and voila, their problem was solved! They were keeping tabs on the time, so they got up and returned to the window, waiting for any movement from Long Haisheng and his family. After Long Haisheng and his family returned from exercising, the nanny went out to the vegetable market, the wife took the child to his tutor, and Long Haisheng left to meet someone with whom he had arranged to have a drink. Chen Sheng and Zhang Guoliang watched these scenes as if they were watching a movie, storing those images away in their brains. Now they had become familiar with the clothing the family wore when they went to exercise and what they looked like in their street clothes as well. Although, they hadn't been able to see their faces clearly, Zhang Guoliang now had a very good idea of what they looked like. If he closed his eyes and tried remembering, he could still conjure up an impression.

The next day was Sunday, and Chen Sheng managed to shepherd Zhang Guoliang through another day. He appealed to Zhang Guoliang to try and buckle down a little, to not let his guard down just because he was becoming accustomed to things. He taught him the saying, 'If you neglect even one per cent, you will one hundred per cent sure to make a mistake'.

He urged Zhang Guoliang to try and knuckle down. Upon meeting Zhang Guoliang this time, Chen Sheng began realising that he was the same old guy that he had always known. It was as if he didn't know what was going on, in some aspects, he even seemed a little stupid or as if nothing really mattered to him. Maybe this foolishness resulted from his poverty, or maybe he really was completely blinded by money. Perhaps this was better, for if Zhang Guoliang was really aware of what he was getting himself into, he might never consider going through with it.

Near the end of their stakeout, Chen Sheng took out a few things he had prepared earlier. These included disguises Zhang Guoliang could use to infiltrate the housing complex, as well as some other dangerous-looking items he could use to frighten the family. Chen Sheng told him, 'We don't want to hurt anybody, it's just that we've run out of other options. We'll use our own ways to get my money back, but let's just not overdo it!'

Chen Sheng then went on to emphasise several key points. 'First of all, we might have to get a little rough on Long Haisheng if we're going to bring him to heel since he is really no angel. Second, his woman and child are the victims here, so there's no point in touching or messing with them. Third, the same goes for the nanny. Best leave the nanny alone and not harm her, for she's just like you in that you both came from the countryside just to try and make a little money in the city, which I'm sure has never been easy for either of you.'

Zhang Guoliang committed these points to memory. The two of them thought that if they planned sufficiently and really thought things out, then they wouldn't have any problem in pulling off their caper.

The Best Time to Enter the Carnival Housing Complex Was at Dusk

That day, Zhang Guoliang was going to enter the Carnival housing complex in the evening at dusk. Chen Sheng felt that this would be the best time to enter since people would be the most distracted and the complex would be at its most vulnerable. Everyone who had been busy outside all day would be returning from all directions back to their nests, while those working inside the complex would have already all changed into their street clothes and would be successively leaving the complex as well. The gardeners, home tutors, managers and office workers inside would have all completed another day of toil by then, and the joyful expressions on their faces as they were leaving would soften the security guards' zeal, making them just a little less attentive to their duties, just a little more perfunctory in their reactions, and this was a time when Zhang Guoliang could surely waltz right in.

Zhang Guoliang dressed as a deliveryman for the Nanwei brand, for a company called Jiangbei Fast Foods. When the security guard stopped him, he asked him, 'Who are you delivering to?'

Zhang Guoliang replied, 'Unit 3 in A Block.'

With that, the security guard simply punched in a code, stepped aside and let Zhang Guoliang inside. The several years Zhang Guoliang had spent in Rezhou served him well, for it was then he had learned how to project that air of seeming nonchalance that Rezhou people had. It was because of his nonchalance that the security guard never really had any reason to doubt him. As Zhang Guoliang rode through the housing complex on his delivery bicycle, the metal case on the back of his bike kept jolting on the flagstone pavement, making a banging sound. At first, Zhang Guoliang was afraid that the sound would attract people's attention, but later discovered the sound to be almost a badge of openness and honesty that completely hid his feelings of awkwardness at being there. The Carnival was truly a very wonderful and beautiful complex. The trees and bushes inside were still lush, even in the dead of winter. The trees and the bushes still had their vibrancy, and both had been planted profusely throughout the complex. *If I am ever forced to flee, this place will provide many convenient places to hide.* The villas themselves were spaced fairly far apart and inconsistently. Chen Sheng had once told him that once he was inside the housing complex, although all the small straight paths were monitored, in the places where the paths curved and twisted, you could dance a jig there and no one would be able to see you. What Zhang Guoliang found most remarkable was people's overall indifference. As Zhang Guoliang glanced around in every direction, it seemed no one paid him any mind. Finally, using a military trick Chen Sheng had taught him, he wrapped an apron around his head so when he came underneath the scrutiny of the CCTV cameras, no one would be able to make out his face. After several noisy laps around the complex and figuring he had sufficiently confused the security cameras by then, Zhang Guoliang screwed up his courage, descended from his bicycle, then rushed directly up to the door of Building 3 in Block A and knocked on Long Haisheng's door. From inside the house, the nanny's voice rang out clearly in response, 'Who's there? Is that property management?'

Zhang Guoliang responded, 'Delivery!'

'Delivery? We aren't expecting any delivery.'

'No? Didn't you order the Fragrant Lotus Brisket Casserole?'

The nanny replied, 'No. I've been here all day and no one's ordered any food.'

Zhang Guoliang then intentionally asked her, 'Isn't this Building 3 in B Block?'

'No, B Block is to the south. It's the third building to the south. This is A Block.'

Zhang Guoliang asked her, 'Madame, which way is south? Can you point it out for me?'

The nanny, becoming annoyed with his questions, peeked through the peephole, and when she saw Zhang Guoliang in his disguise and his 'Junior' name tag, she simply opened the door and stepped out. This was when Zhang Guoliang charged forward, squeezed past her and managed to get himself inside the house. When the nanny screamed, Zhang Guoliang ripped off his overcoat to reveal the row of dynamite sticks taped tightly to his chest. The sticks of dynamite were as thick as Rezhou's speciality blood sausage, and were as long as those sausages as well. They were wrapped in a newspaper, eight in a row, and they extended from one armpit across his chest to the other. They looked powerful and frightening. Zhang Guoliang also held a remote control in his hand that emitted a dazzling red light when he lightly pressed its button. Zhang Guoliang directed the nanny in a slow and measured voice, telling her, 'Shut up! Scream again and I'll blow this house to kingdom come!'

It all was proceeding precisely as Chen Sheng had imagined, precisely as he had planned. The nanny shut her mouth, then raised her hands as if in surrender, but also as if to signal to someone else who was there. The child doing her homework in the dining room immediately saw what was happening, then Long Haisheng's wife, who was sitting by her side, became aware of it too. Zhang Guoliang barked, 'Get the man of the house here right now!'

The nanny explained, 'He's upstairs.'

Zhang Guoliang ordered, 'Then tell him to come downstairs!'

The wife, pointing to the little girl asked, 'Should I call him, or should she?'

This was when the child burst out, 'Daddy! Come downstairs! Someone's here to see you!'

Zhang Guoliang then heard the sound of feet leisurely padding down some stairs. The first thing that came into his view was a pair of feet in some slippers, then a dark-coloured floral-patterned velvet nightgown, and then finally a face that had turned white with astonishment. Both men looked at each other at the same moment. When Long Haisheng saw Zhang Guoliang, he thought him slightly comical, since he was wearing clothes from a take-out restaurant while at the same time had a bomb strapped to his chest. When Zhang Guoliang saw the dapper Long Haisheng, he thought, *He somehow seems different from the man we were spying on! He looks almost like someone who might be my trusted advisor!*

Long Haisheng indeed gave the impression of being a trusted advisor. He told him serenely 'Friend, whatever you need, let's talk about it. Whatever you're doing now is useless.'

Zhang Guoliang retorted, 'Don't waste your breath. This is the only way to deal with someone like you!'

He ordered them all into the living room, and following his instructions, they all went in and sat on the couch. Zhang Guoliang directed the nanny to tie them up according to plan. The nanny hesitated at first, looking awkwardly at Long Haisheng who told her, 'Listen to him and do whatever he says. Don't resist.' The nanny went over to a cupboard by the door. Although the cupboard was messy, she found some cotton rope, some electrical cord, and finally a roll of tape. Zhang Guoliang told her, 'Use that.'

According to Chen Sheng's instructions, Zhang Guoliang had the nanny tape Long Haisheng's hands behind his back and his wife's hands in front of her. When it came to the child and the nanny, Zhang Guoliang thought, one was just a child and the other was just like him. His heart softened and he let them be. Now that the situation was under his control, his mind began to settle down. In an authoritative voice he wasn't used to using, he began telling the family what he intended to do. 'First, the remote control in my hand is very sensitive, and it works extremely well. Do you see this flickering red button? All I have to do is press it lightly and this entire building will immediately be blown to smithereens. Second, don't think that by some fluke I won't be able to detonate my bomb. We have mines where I come from and I've been blowing up rocks in those mines since I was a kid. I am very good at this. Third, I am not doing anything underhanded. I am not a thief, nor a kidnapper, nor an extortionist. I'm here to collect a debt for someone. That's right! Isn't there someone you owe money to? Of course, there is. I wouldn't be here if there wasn't! I'm not here by accident. Fourth, I won't hurt the child, you can rest assured, but you adults had better tow the line and behave. If you act out, or you try and trick me, or use some ruse, then I'm afraid you'll never have time to even regret it. Fifth, Nanny, you need to listen to me, for you're in the same boat as I am. I don't want to make your life any more difficult, but I'm going to need you to help me. I want the rest of our time together to pass as peacefully as possible, but you are the ones who hold all of our fates in your hands. Do you understand what I'm telling you?'

The nanny didn't dare to even blink, but simply nodded her head as if her life depended on it. Long Haisheng spoke up then and asked, 'Will you at least tell me who you are collecting the debt for?'

Zhang Guoliang said, 'Look how you are still so crafty even now! Do you really think I will let on to you who sent me? Try being a little more honest with yourself. Are you really telling me that you've never reneged on a debt? Think about it, if I were here to rob or extort you, would I really be this polite to you? I would've blown you up long ago. All I can tell you is, that after I have the money all neatly in hand, I won't keep you guessing any longer.'

It was seven in the evening by then, and a cosiness began gradually pervading the housing complex air. Yet, for the family Zhang Guoliang had intruded on and was harassing, it felt like they were enveloped in an oppressive haze. Long Haisheng sat begrudgingly upon the couch with his hands tied behind his back looking very uncomfortable. His wife too leaned listlessly against the couch, staring woodenly at her own bound hands. Right then she was surely thinking, *I'm going to have to try to become a better person from now on!* The child snuggled closely to her mother's side, blinking her eyes curiously. Perhaps she was thinking that Zhang Guoliang was not really as fiendish as he seemed.

The nanny had already gone into the kitchen to prepare something to eat, and although she seemed to be going about it conscientiously, you could tell that her heart was really not in it. This was Zhang Guoliang's idea for her to make some food. He told them, 'Life must go on.'

Not thinking much of it, he told her, 'All I want is a cup of instant noodles.'

This was also part of Chen Sheng's plan. He had decided that after they had the family under control, they would then take it easy on them. What they had more than anything else of that evening was time. The longer the time dragged out, the greater the pressure they would feel, the more likely they would cave and the closer the plan would come to succeeding. All else was very normal in the Carnival housing complex. As the night began falling, the gentle music of the earth began spiralling up through the underbrush and the soft lights of the complex began spreading out through the sky. There was the occasional sound of a car or pedestrian passing by, but otherwise, it was just another quiet, rainy night. Finishing his noodles, Zhang Guoliang suddenly stood up and said, 'I want to go upstairs to have a look and see if everything is safe.'

He went on, saying, 'This bomb around my chest is too heavy. I want to take it off and put it in the safest place in your house.'

He wanted Long Haisheng to show him the way. He told the others, 'You stay downstairs and behave. Do what you like, but don't go AWOL on me, ok? I know you all love this house and love living here the way you do, so I'm telling you, if by the time your husband and I get back down here, it will just be a few minutes, if one of you is not here in the living room when we return, then I'll have no choice but to blow up the house. It'll go puff and then be gone.'

As Zhang Guoliang spoke, he suddenly exclaimed, 'Oh! I just remembered something! Your cell phones! Everyone, give me your phones!'

Long Haisheng told his family, 'Listen to him! Hurry up and give him your phones!'

Long Haisheng took the lead, shaking his hips to indicate that his cell phone was beneath his nightgown. Zhang Guoliang unceremoniously reached into his pocket and fished out the phone. Next, he took the wife's phone and then the nanny's. When he came to the child, the nanny told him, 'The child has no phone.'

In this case, Zhang Guoliang chose to believe her. After collecting the phones, he put them all in the kitchen sink, then began filling the sink with water. This too was Chen Sheng's idea. He said, 'If you cut them off from the outside world, then you will own them and your troubles will be behind you.'

Long Haisheng obediently led the way upstairs for Zhang Guoliang. Zhang Guoliang wanted to know if there was anything upstairs that he should be concerned about. Chen Sheng had felt that since Zhang Guoliang was going through so much trouble, he might as well be absolutely sure. The villa's design had been well thought out. The staircase was in the centre of the house with bedrooms on each floor extending out like the petals on a flower. The house was decorated in a European style, with vases placed at the foot of each staircase, and large oil paintings hanging in the alcoves. Zhang Guoliang knew nothing about oil paintings, but he felt that their style did not harmonise well with the rest of the house. They were simple paintings of flowers and plants, painted in the warm colours of the countryside. At Zhang Guoliang's behest, they first went up to the loft on the top floor.

Zhang Guoliang quietly warned Long Haisheng, 'Get any illusions of trying to overpower me out of your head, for you'll be no match for me in a fight! Besides, you don't have much strength in your leg, do you?'

When Long Haisheng heard this, he was taken aback. Zhang Guoliang just stood there smirking.

The loft had been fashioned into a kind of a home movie theatre, and to make it soundproof, the entire loft had mostly been sealed up tight. Zhang Guoliang ordered him to turn off the lights, shut the door and lock it. Long Haisheng did each of these in turn as he was told, never daring to omit even one.

They returned to the third floor where the bedrooms were located. There were Long Haisheng and his wife's, the nanny's, the child's, and an additional guest bedroom prepared for relatives when they occasionally visited. Zhang Guoliang made a beeline over to Long Haisheng's bed, felt around beneath the pillows, then pulled out a short sword, a formidable one, like the one used by the Yue emperors. This one, however, was clearly meant for business. Again, Long Haisheng was astonished. Zhang Guoliang told him frankly, 'I'm not stupid. I know all about your past.'

People said that Long Haisheng had a habit left over from the days when he used to fight, that he slept with a sword under his pillow. Before Long Haisheng regained his senses, Zhang Guoliang told him, 'I'll put the bomb beneath your bed! We'll take it out as soon as you hand over the money. Otherwise, I may just have to set it off!'

Long Haisheng asked him directly, 'Who are you collecting for? If you're collecting on a debt, you need to tell me how much it's for if you want me to get it! Stop jacking me around like this!'

Zhang Guoliang retorted, 'Ok, I'll tell you what I want! I want 450 000 *yuan*, and you'd better find a way to get it!'

Long Haisheng repeated, '450 000 *yuan*? I don't have 450 000 *yuan*! Who has that much cash lying around? The most I have on hand is 50 or 60 thousand.'

Zhang Guoliang thought, Chen Sheng was right! These people all have money lying around. Cheng Sheng had told him that they sometimes liked to gamble at home, and they always used cash when they did. Whether they won or lost, they always had tens of thousands in cash stashed away at home.

Now that Zhang Guoliang had him at sword-point, Long Haisheng had no choice but to lead him over to a wastebasket and point to it. The wastebasket was in a corner of the room, under a rack of clothes, and inside it were crumpled tissues, empty cookie packages and empty candied-fruit boxes. These were used as camouflage, for underneath them were piles of cash. Zhang Guoliang gasped, then disdainfully picked up the wastebasket.

On the second floor was a tearoom with a bar and a mahjong table. There were bottles of liquor lining the walls, and bottles of red wine stacked like artillery shells on the floor. The lavish decoration of the place bedazzled Zhang Guoliang, but he was not there to take a tour or to dawdle. He had a mission to carry out. Starting from the movie theatre in the fourth-floor loft above, they turned off all the lights and shut the windows on each floor as they came down. The villa also came equipped with 'firewalls', sliding steel doors that shut off every staircase. As Zhang Guoliang slid these shut as they descended, sealing off every floor, it was like he was locking all the danger outside. Now, a dejected Long Haisheng, escorted by Zhang Guoliang at sword point, returned to the living room on the first floor.

When the child saw the sword, she exclaimed, 'That's my father's sword! What are you doing with it?'

Zhang Guoliang replied, 'He let me borrow it to play with for a bit. I'll give it back to him soon.'

All that seemed to remain now of that 300 or 400 square meter villa was the living room on the first floor. With Long Haisheng's assistance, all of the other rooms had been locked down. If one didn't know any better and looked in from outside, it would have seemed as if the whole family was going about having dinner in the first-floor living room, as if no one had begun going about their business upstairs, since everything was dark. With the villa locked down like this, there remained only one entrance going in or out. All Zhang Guoliang had to do now was to watch them all closely. He was now in a position where he could call all the shots.

During those few minutes they had spent going up and down the stairs, the women and the child had remained obediently upon the couch. Zhang Guoliang could see that the very moment he arrived downstairs. They were all very cooperative and were sure to listen to what he said, for they were afraid of the detonator he held in his hand.

Zhang Guoliang had Long Haisheng sit down as well, then began carefully counting out the money. He was neither a thief nor an extortionist. He was just following someone's orders to collect on a debt. He had a responsibility to the man above him, for they had an agreement. Even if it was just a verbal agreement, still, it was an agreement among gentlemen. They had agreed that if Zhang Guoliang brought back the 300 000 *yuan*, then he would receive 10 per cent. His boss was trusting him with every penny, and what he brought back to him would ultimately determine how much he himself would make.

He asked himself, *When had he ever seen so much money?* Never. He had no idea how many bills were in each bundle, or if there were a set number of bills in each. He took the garbage can and dumped its contents out all over the dining room table. There were five bundles and some loose notes as well in the mix, all folded and bound with rubber bands. He placed the sword he had confiscated by his left hand, and the detonator down by his right just in case anything happened and he needed to get to them fast. He tore off the rubber band from one of the bundles and began counting the notes. Of course, he couldn't count them like a bank teller would, for he had never counted out so much money before and he easily made mistakes. He could only count them note by note until he reached ten, then put them in a pile, count out another ten, then put them in another pile. He often lost count and had to start all over again. Long Haisheng and his family watched from a distance at him counting. Zhang Guoliang made them nervous. They couldn't wait for him to stop counting, to just take the money and go.

The nanny told him dryly, 'There's no need to count it. There's 10 000 *yuan* in each bundle. There's 50 or 60 thousand there. Just take it and go.'

Zhang Guoliang told her, 'That's not gonna fly, sister. I still haven't completed my mission!'

He first told Long Haisheng he wanted 450 000 *yuan*, so that he wouldn't be able to guess who had sent him. What he was actually planning on getting was the 300 000 *yuan*. What was 60 000 *yuan* compared with that? He could never go back to Chen Sheng with only 60 000 *yuan*, and if he took the 60 000 and left right away, then it really would be considered robbery. Only when he had the full 300 000 *yuan* would he be able to consider his mission completed and realise his ambition to return home.

He turned to the nanny and said, 'This will do for today. Go find me a bag for me, then stuff this money inside.'

Why was the Carnival Housing Complex on TV?

Chen Sheng was just like Zhang Guoliang in that all he had eaten that day was a bowl of instant noodles. When he kept thinking about Zhang Guoliang and what he might be up to at that moment, he lost his appetite and couldn't eat. Instant noodles were not much more than water anyway; you just boiled them to cook them, and after they cooled, you could just pick up the bowl and quickly slurp them down.

Chen Sheng imagined Zhang Guoliang going through the entire procedure, from him entering the house, intimidating the family, gathering them together, tying them up, eating, inspecting the house then closing it off, then counting the money. Everything would have taken time, and if it all went smoothly including negotiating with the family and making his reasons clear to them,

Zhang Guoliang should have finished up before 8 p.m. He would have returned home in triumph by 8.30.

If he'd fought and been bloodied, he might not have dared to take a cab, then he would've had to thread his way through the lanes and back alleys, which might have added another half hour. Even if taking that into account, he should still have been back already.

It was now 10 in the evening and there was still no word from Zhang Guoliang. Chen Sheng was more than 80 per cent sure this meant that something had gone wrong. *What could possibly have gone wrong?* Zhang Guoliang was a farm hand, which meant he was physically very strong. Even if Long Haisheng and even his entire family had tried to jump him and beat him, they may still not have been a match for him.

Otherwise, perhaps the family had been on guard from the start, and as soon as Zhang Guoliang set foot in the house, they caught him in some trap they had set, and they now had him bound and tied. This was not beyond the range of possibilities.

How did he expect the naïve and clumsy Zhang Guoliang to ever be a match for that crafty Long Haisheng? Perhaps at that very moment, Long Haisheng was trying Zhang Guoliang in some makeshift court that he had set up. A man with Long Haisheng's personality would never have handed Zhang Guoliang directly over to the police. He would have been certain toy with him, to torment him. Chen Sheng couldn't imagine how he would torture Zhang Guoliang, he only knew that he would never make it easy for him. He would try to get him to open his mouth, get him to spill the beans. Who put you up to this? Who is your ringleader?

If that were to happen, would Zhang Guoliang really sell him out? Chen Sheng thought, Never! Zhang Guoliang was way too trustworthy for that!

That year he had mistakenly sent him down to the police station, when Zhang Guoliang had been wrongly interrogated under torture, he had remained by Chen Sheng's side when he had gotten out. This showed the importance Zhang Guoliang placed on camaraderie. Anyway, they had already been out of touch for many years now, and if it had been he who had brought Zhang Guoliang to Rezhou, nobody had seen them together since they had never gone outside. Zhang Guoliang wouldn't have any of Chen Sheng's personal information on him, so even if he did talk, he couldn't say much that would be significant. It would all be too confusing, and in any case, no one would necessarily believe him.

Maybe Long Haisheng was scrolling through Zhang Guoliang's cell phone to see who he had most recently contacted. As things stood then, the easiest way information could be revealed was through his cell phone. Chen Sheng had been aware of this from the very beginning, so he never once used his cell phone to contact

Zhang Guoliang. He had been more than willing to take a little more trouble to do everything he had to do personally without ever using his cell.

If you wanted to trace communications between his cell and Zhang Guoliang's, you'd have to go back many years to that time when he was his boss. You would have to go back all the way back to when Zhang Guoliang was working for him processing scraps, to the time when he had called him during the Spring Festival and urged him to come back as soon as he could to work. That was the only time they had been in touch with each other by cell, and their conversations back then had been brief.

When are you coming back?

Next week.

If I give you money for your travel expenses, can you hurry back here by tomorrow night?

Ok, I can do that!

That was it, they had never spoken for long.

Chen Sheng once heard that information was kept on an ordinary cell phone for three years, and that anyone could check traces of calls and messages going back three years by scrolling through it. Chen Sheng thought, *This must especially be done to keep tabs on party members. Party members were at the greatest risk, and this was probably done as a way to monitor them.* Why on earth would an ordinary person ever need to go back that far? What would be gained from it? All those telephone calls that everyone all over the world was making to everyone else; what was the use in knowing all that?? You'd be overwhelmed by the sheer quantity of that information in a matter of moments!

Even though Zhang Guoliang had a cell phone, the telephone number he was using might not even be real. People from the countryside were inherently crafty, they knew to protect themselves. They loved using fake ID cards to buy disposable telephone numbers. Who was to say that even his name, Zhang Guoliang, wasn't a fake…

No way! That couldn't be! Nothing so unlucky could happen to me! Bad things generally happened to bad people, to swindlers or shysters, meaning if anyone should be having bad luck, then it should be Long Haisheng! No, no… I've got to stop, it's too early to start thinking like this!

Well then, could Zhang Guoliang still be waiting on the cash? This was entirely possible. He was so honest and so stubborn that he would be sure to do what he was told to do. If you told him to go and get 300 000, then that was how much he would be sure to come back with. Chen Sheng had made it clear to him that someone like Long Haisheng would always be sure to have a certain amount of cash on hand at home. That he might not have the entire 300 000 in cash on hand was a problem he neglected to consider. In any case, Zhang Guoliang may have already gotten his hands on a lesser amount of cash, and having gotten a first sweet taste of victory, he was perhaps now holding out for even more cash. Of course, all of this was speculation on Cheng Sheng's part. Whatever Zhang Guoliang was actually doing, he had no way of really knowing.

Zhang Guoliang was indeed waiting on the money. He was sure that facts would prove they were going about things in the right way. Some folks were just like Long Haisheng, they never shed a tear until they saw a coffin, they'd cut off their nose to spite their face. If you didn't lean hard on them, they'd never compromise.

From whatever angle you looked at it, how could Chen Sheng ever consider this to be easy money? As a business calculus, he should have been earning 8 per cent on his money. He figured he was now in to the tune of 300 000, but probably more than 290 000 of that had been his original capital. This didn't even take into account the amount of blood, sweat and tears as a businessman he had put into servicing the debt, and all he was trying to recover was the 300 000 *yuan*! Do you think Long Haisheng ever gave a single thought to any of this?

Vicious and merciless people like him only knew how to lean on people, to swindle them, then kick them when they're down. *He would've reneged on both the principal and interest. I'm not gonna let him get away with it!* This is why Chen Sheng and Zhang Guoliang had to go to such extremes in dealing with him, why they had to resort to such primitive methods, to weaponry and explosives. Only these things could keep him in line, so when you told him to sit, he dared not stand, or when you told him to eat, he dared not drink.

Zhang Guoliang asked him, 'How could you think that 60 000 *yuan* would ever do? Do you think my boss sent a child to do an adult's job? I could never go back to him with only 60 000 *yuan*.'

When Zhang Guoliang had finished counting the money, he returned to sit opposite Long Haisheng and his family, the remote control in one hand and the bag of money in the other. As Long Haisheng, his family and the nanny sat before him, he could feel the disparity of power between them, how the advantage was indeed still on Zhang Guoliang's side.

He told them patiently, 'This dispute between us is not a question of who wronged whom. It all comes down to the question of money.'

Zhang Guoliang continued, 'It may have been a question of right and wrong at the start, but that's no longer an issue. It might have been different if you had paid your debts like you should have, then there would've been no question of right and wrong. We wouldn't be having a dispute like this one now, and I wouldn't be here interrupting your lives. So, it's not like I'm making life difficult for you, but more like you should be doing the right thing and helping me out.'

Long Haisheng told him, 'I know you might not believe me, but right now I really don't have any more money on hand. You've already taken the little money I had. What else do you want from me?'

Zhang Guoliang replied, 'It isn't what else I want from you, you haven't given me anything yet. Do you think just because you have no money on hand now that I should just forget all about it? If you don't have any more money here, then go and borrow some from your friends!'

Long Haisheng exclaimed, 'You've soaked all of our phones! How am I supposed to call anyone?'

Zhang Guoliang replied condescendingly, 'I had no choice but to soak your phones. If I hadn't, it would've been too dangerous for me since I would never have been able to control you. That won't be a problem now anyway, since I have my own phone. It may not be a good one, but it will still make calls with no problem.'

With that, Zhang Guoliang fished out his cell phone from his pocket. You could see that it was an old Nokia, perhaps one that someone had previously discarded. When he flipped opened the phone, he discovered that he had foolishly let it run out of power. A cell phone like this never originally had much battery capacity, but he had forgotten to charge it due to his nervousness while making preparations. It didn't matter though, for he had a way of dealing with even such an adverse circumstance as this.

One year, Chen Sheng jokingly told him about some survival tips he had learned while he was in the army, one of which was how to charge a cell phone. Zhang Guoliang told Long Haisheng to wait while he went into the bathroom. Without closing the door, so he could hear and know what was going on in the living room, he then began urinating on the cell phone. His stream of urine was long and it stank, but seemed to work just like a highly concentrated medicine and had an immediate effect on the cell phone. Chen Sheng had never explained the reason why it worked. Perhaps urine contained some special component. In any case, when he next opened his cell, it started right up.

Zhang Guoliang went back over to Long Haisheng, and when Long Haisheng repeated a telephone number to him, Zhang Guoliang dialed it and put the phone up to Long Haisheng's ear. At the start of the call, Long Haisheng began murmuring, as if he was trying to speak in code, but when Zhang Guoliang started waving the remote control in front of his face, Long Haisheng quickly shaped up. He began fabricating excuses for why he needed money, saying that wages were due at his factory tomorrow or that he had to pay off a loan that was due and so forth. Long Haisheng repeated everything the other party was saying in order to convey it back to Zhang Guoliang.

Who keeps cash like that at home now? All our large amounts are now done by electronic transfer! I have the money, just not that much on hand! I've got to find some way to get it and have it sent over here by tomorrow morning!'

Long Haisheng added, 'It's night now. Even if you tried calling the bank, you wouldn't get any money!'

Zhang Guoliang thought about it and then realised he was right. He thought, *Tonight is bound to be a long and grueling one.*

That evening, Chen Sheng learned what it meant 'to become bored to death'. He tried imagining what might be happening down at the Carnival. He had been the one who had come up with the plan, but whether Zhang Guoliang was carrying it out as he directed or was deviating from it in any way, he could only imagine as a way to dispel the impatience and confusion he was feeling at that time. In his boredom, he turned on the TV. There was nothing in particular that he wanted to watch, there was just nothing else to do, and he wanted to kill time.

In most inns like the one they were in, there was no satellite TV, but only local channels, so he turned to the local Rezhou news channel. Just then, at 10 p.m., a broadcast called *On the Spot News* was just beginning. On the TV screen, there was a picture of a housing complex with several police cars stopped in front of its gate. Their red and blue lights were flashing silently while a few policemen who looked like brass stood huddled around whispering to each other. The camera then began panning from the front gate to the inside of the complex where a section had been cordoned off with police tape, and officers were directing people to keep clear of a path that led to several villas sitting serenely in the darkness. *Why did those villas seem so familiar?*

The pattern on the front gate he just saw seemed familiar as well, and the road leading inside the complex also seemed familiar. Chen Sheng thought, *If only it were daytime and if only the camera would stay still for a minute, I would surely recognise where that housing complex is.*

Rezhou had several compounds of nice villas all built by people from Hong Kong and Taiwan. As the aesthetic and planning concepts were different in those two places, naturally their housing complexes were laid out differently as well. Chen Sheng could see it was in the Taiwanese style, but he couldn't put his finger on the design. It was traditional, in a simple style.

He continued analysing it in his mind until it suddenly dawned on him. *Isn't that the Carnival housing complex? What's going on there? How could it be? What was happening inside the compound? Was there a fire?* Yet, there was no sign of any fire. *Perhaps some cars had clipped each other on the road and there was an accident?*

Yet, there was no sign of any argument going on inside. *Had a child slipped and fallen into the pond?* There was no sign of any chaos, nor was there any din of crying inside.

Chen Sheng then became aware that there didn't even appear to be any sound coming from the TV. Even the ordinarily conspicuous sound of police sirens seemed to be absent. There was only an image on the screen. *How could this be? Why were they being so quiet?* There could only be one answer. This was no ordinary television program – it was a live broadcast. They were recording the police going about their work in real time, as if they were on some kind of top-secret mission. They could only have one purpose, they were dealing with a suspect that had already infiltrated someone's home and they wanted to keep him totally in the dark as to their presence. They were surrounding Zhang Guoliang without giving him the slightest inkling they were doing so. This could only mean that Zhang Guoliang's operation had already been exposed.

Chen Sheng immediately got himself up and rushed over to the Carnival, but he hesitated once he approached the front gate. When he looked on from a distance at the housing complex, he saw many people surrounding the gate seemingly discussing things as they went about watching. He really wanted to go over to hear what they were saying, to find out what was going on, to see if things were really happening as he imagined them.

If it was like he imagined, then he wanted badly to get inside the villa to warn Zhang Guoliang! That way Zhang Guoliang could at least heighten his vigilance, proceed even more cautiously, keep his head down and quit earlier than planned if he had to. Even if this proved not to be the case, even if Chen Sheng was being overly nervous, it would never hurt Zhang Guoliang to be more cautious and more vigilant, but with things as they stood now, how could Chen Sheng ever get inside? What would he say to the security guards at the gate? How would he ever get through the police cordon? How would he ever get close to Building No 3 in A Block?

If things were truly as they seemed, at what point had they slipped-up so that Zhang Guoliang had now been exposed? Chen Sheng thought, *Firstly, Zhang Guoliang shouldn't have had any problem with the procedure, with tying up the adults, with soaking the phones, with locking the front door, with closing off the corridors or with gathering everyone together – the entire plan had been watertight! Secondly, we had explained our motivations to the family very clearly. We explained that we'd been forced into collecting the debt this way, that we had no other choice. We'd never entered their home to rob, kidnap or blackmail them, and most importantly we'd never intended to injure anyone in the process of sequestering them. They should have clearly understood our motivations by then. Thirdly, the fact that we never took the money and ran spoke for itself. If we had just taken what we could have and then left, then you could indeed describe this as bandit-like behaviour, but we waited around, hoping the family would come to their senses, hoping they would discover their conscience. Now, there was no way of turning back the clock, and things are developing for us in a very unfavourable direction. Where had we slipped-up to start things turning against us like this?*

There was no way any of the family would have time to slip off, for they had mostly remained within the range of Zhang Guoliang's watchful eye. Could Long Haisheng, while pretending to cooperate by turning off the lights, have in fact triggered some kind of an emergency alarm that directly alerted the police? Had he installed a fire alarm in his villa, a burglar alarm, and some kind of emergency alarm as well? Perhaps he had some special installation that an outsider would have no way of knowing about. It seemed like Zhang Guoliang should have had the upper hand, but had Long Haisheng, in fact, tricked him and reported him to the police without him ever even knowing it? None of this speculation was beyond the range of possibilities!

Chen Sheng recalled an event in the past when he had once gone to Shanghai to restock his supplies. His supplier there was polite enough to arrange for him to stay in a new house in Pudong. It was a really luxurious house with a view of the river, but Chen Sheng felt out of place, like some kind of country bumpkin. He woke at night for some inexplicable reason, then decided that he needed to pee. He then wanted to have look around the other rooms, and go out on the balcony to have a look down at the Bund, but he couldn't find the right switches to turn on the lights. As he flipped through those different switches, he inadvertently triggered an alarm without even knowing it. A short while later, someone knocked on the door, and when he looked through the peephole, he saw a group of security guards standing in the doorway. Stunned, he opened the door to the security guards, and one them asked him, 'Did something happen here?'

Chen Sheng replied, 'No, why?'

The security guard told him, 'Someone triggered the alarm!'

Completely puzzled, he said 'Huh? I triggered an alarm?'

Of course, they left satisfied after they heard his explanation.

Could Long Haisheng's villa have an installation like this as well? What kind of alarm could he have possibly tripped? A fire alarm? A burglar alarm? Could there have been another kind of emergency alarm? It stood to reason that if an alarm had in fact been triggered, then security would have first come to the door to investigate. Now, not only were the police directly involved, but they also were deliberately trying not to alarm anyone in Building 3 in A Block. Furthermore, they were in the process of stealthily surrounding the building. Clearly, he had not just triggered the switch of any old alarm. Clearly, the report the police had of what was going on inside was not vague, but in fact very accurate-someone had broken in and taken hostages, someone with explosives and weapons. So, after discussing the measures they should take, the police decided not to try and take the suspect head on by force, but to try and think of another ruse by which to outsmart him.

Chen Sheng racked his brains trying to think, *Where had the plan gone wrong?* As he went back over everything step by step, he suddenly became so alarmed that he broke out in a cold sweat all over. *Was it the child? It would have been easiest to overlook the child. Zhang Guoliang had forced Long Haisheng to hand over his cell phone and had confiscated the wife's and nanny's cell phones as well, but perhaps he overlooked the fact that the child may have had a phone!*

Zhang Guoliang may have never even imagined that the child would have had a phone! In fact, most of the children in Rezhou already had their own cell phones. By the time they started school, or by the time they spent any time on their own, their parents made sure they had cell phones. How good a phone it was depended on the parents. They might have a Little Smartphone, or perhaps just an ordinary phone, but for a family like Long Haisheng's, if the child had really wanted it, it was possible she may have even had an iPhone 4. If this was the case, then maybe when Zhang Guoliang escorted Long Haisheng to busy themselves upstairs, the child may have mischievously taken out her cell phone to call. Any child of Long Haisheng's would be sure to be full of piss and vinegar like that. Maybe her mother told her to go hide in the bathroom and call the police. Maybe the mother had stayed in the living room keeping watch while the child and the nanny dashed into the bathroom. Maybe then the child took out her cell phone, gave it to the nanny, and the nanny explained the goings on there to the police. She would not have been able, in that critical moment, to go into much detail or be that precise. She wouldn't have gone into any of the details at all; she would have only told them they were being robbed. She wouldn't have said anything about the robber's story; she would have only told them that he had a bomb. She might have even exaggerated, adding a detail or two of her own; maybe about how he had terrible weapons or maybe she even told them he had a shiny black handgun, or something like that! When people report to the police, experience suggests that they always report their situation as being more threatening than it really is out of fear they will not garner enough of police's attention. If it was like Chen Sheng imagined, then the way the nanny reported the incident would clearly have turned the case into a frame-up; turned what was originally a debt collection into a robbery. This would be much more serious for Zhang Guoliang, since it would change the entire nature of the case.

It would only have taken the nanny and the kid a few short minutes to report to the police and then make it back to the couch by the time Zhang Guoliang and Long Haisheng had come downstairs. The three girls would have appeared well-behaved, like they had been sitting there the whole time as they looked up at Zhang Guoliang trembling in fear and trepidation. Maybe he was getting careless, or maybe he was letting his initial success go to his head, but Zhang Guoliang might never have noticed anything at all to be amiss.

Chen Sheng then regretted the one thing he never told him before they started! Before they started, all he told Zhang Guoliang was a proverb: 'A lame wolf finds it difficult to fight'. The thing he neglected to tell him was a line from a movie that went, 'The one who sells you out is usually just like you.'

It was always possible that the queer happenings

inside the housing complex had nothing to do with Zhang Guoliang, that it was some other emergency, or that it was some other accident. There was no way for Chen Sheng to be sure, but he was hoping this might be the case.

The Housing Complex was Gloomy, Though Its Lights Burnt Brightly

In the living room in Building 3 in A Block, it was Long Haisheng's turn to contend with Zhang Guoliang, the topic still being the debt. Long Haisheng made a great show of wanting to use Zhuang Guoliang's phone so that he could contact several other people. Long Haisheng complained bitterly, telling him it wasn't that he was unwilling to repay the debt, it was just that he was doing what everyone else did. If they thought they could get away with owing someone else money, then that is what they would do. Every day they could get away without paying was a good day.

Zhang Guoliang said, 'You'd never have paid in the end.'

Long Haisheng told him, 'This is just how business is done here in Rezhou. I was just going with the flow, doing what the others were doing. That way, I didn't have to rack my brain too much.'

Zhang Guoliang replied, 'That's why the market is so chaotic, because of people like you, people like you who never follow the rules.'

Long Haisheng argued, 'I used to always pay my debts on time before, but then people started owing me money. Who's to say I can't I owe them money too?'

Zhang Guoliang told him, 'You're so smug and self-righteous, but you really don't get it, do you? How could anyone do business if everyone were like you?'

Long Haisheng replied, 'You can't force anyone to do business. If you're going to do business, then you will need to go along to get along.'

Zhang Guoliang said dryly, 'You talk just like a gangster, and that's why I'd really take pleasure in blowing you up!'

A while later, Long Haisheng's daughter wanted to watch the television. She said her teacher had told them that at 10 p.m. that evening they would be airing a show about their school's art festival. Zhang Guoliang let her turn on the television. When she turned on the TV, no picture jumped up on the screen the way it usually did – it didn't go to any program. All that appeared on the screen was the manufacturer's logo. After a moment, the manufacturer's logo disappeared and the words, 'no signal input' abruptly appeared in the corner of the screen. The police had in fact cut off the TV signal from the outside long ago, their objective being to cut off Building 3 in Block A, so they couldn't see the situation unfolding outside. They wanted to isolate them.

Zhang Guoliang dim-wittedly remarked, 'I wonder if it's a bad outside connection? Shall we call the management office and see?'

Long Haisheng, perhaps already well aware of what was going on outside, knowing the situation that was developing there, deliberately said, 'Never mind. Let's forget about it.'

At 11 that evening, Zhang Guoliang thought about sleeping. In any case, the money wouldn't be there until morning. How would he get through that endless night? Should he let them all go upstairs to rest? No, that would make them too difficult to control. He would never be able to keep an eye on them, he would never know what they were up to. What if they were to signal or make contact with someone on the outside? Then he would be finished. The family could stay in the living room just as they had until then so he could keep an eye on their each and every move, so they wouldn't try to cook up some scheme. The couches would have to make do for them to get some sleep.

Zhang Guoliang told them, 'The child can sleep on the couch. Tomorrow, she still needs to go to school. You'll all just have to make do. Anyway, I'll be here with you right up till the end. When you sit, I'll be sitting too. When you lie down, I'll still be sitting. This is no picnic for me either. I hope none of you will do anything foolish and that we can all try to cooperate in getting peacefully through the night.'

Zhang Guoliang then told the nanny to turn off the lights, but to leave a small light on in the bathroom and leave the door open a little so it wouldn't be too bright. It made the room feel smaller, made everyone feel closer together, made them feel safer.

Zhang Guoliang, wanting to have one last quick inspection, went over to the front door. First, he cocked his ear to listen, then he looked out through the peep-hole. The police had in fact made sure long before that nothing outside was out of place. He could see a bamboo garden, its bamboo gently swaying. On the other side was a fishpond. Its water was stagnant, but the light reflecting off the duckweed on its surface created a soft and mellow ambiance.

To Zhang Guoliang's left was another bathroom, its door shut tightly. To the right was the kitchen. In it was only a small ventilation window, the blades of the electric ventilation fan turning slowly. Behind the couch were two-tiered French windows made from hardened steel, and beyond them lay an exquisite hand railing. Zhang Guoliang stealthily lifted the curtain up a crack to look outside. Opposite the villa there was a clubhouse that rented out rooms called the Vientiane Pavilion. It was not open to the general public, but the boss would use it when a few of his friends would come by to drink tea, listen to the Chinese zither, paint or to practice Chinese calligraphy. That night the clubhouse was serenely bathed in yellow candlelight and enveloped by the sounds of a Chinese zither as usual.

Everything seemed safe and sound. Zhang Guoliang just needed to wait for the time to pass. He just needed to wait for the arrival of daylight.

Chen Sheng saw all this, however, as the calm before the storm, the lull before the battle. If his guess was not mistaken, the police would already be evacuating the residents by now, especially those living nearby to Building 3 in A Block. They police would be working right now, going from house to house, trying to persuade everyone to evacuate. *What excuse would they give for them having to evacuate*? he wondered. The police could not, of course, tell them there was bomb in the area, for that would just incite panic and even cause resentment among the residents. Their best excuse would be to say that they'd discovered there was some contagious disease going around, something like SARS, or the bird flu. The residents in that luxury complex lived comfortable and easy lives. They all loved living at Carnival. They would be sure to take any news you broke to them very seriously, but you had to break it to them gently. If you calmly and collectedly ask them to gradually withdraw, they might just take off like a bat out of hell.

No one could blame the police for wanting to evacuate the residents. They had received a report that someone had a bomb made of eight sticks of dynamite as thick and long as sausages, dynamite like they used in the mines. They estimated the device to be so powerful that the expression 'raze to the ground' immediately came to the mind of even the most unsophisticated person. Since the police didn't want Zhang Guoliang to raze them and everything else around them to the ground, they had to make sure they had a surefire plan, that their arrangements would be flawless. Whatever could be seen through the peephole in Building 3 in A Block, whatever could be seen from the window, whether it was the bamboo garden or the fish pond by the door, the flower beds in the back, or the clubhouse, everything had to seem normal and peaceful, as if nothing were out of the ordinary.

The police had, of course, considered how difficult it might be to wait until nightfall to try and take the house by storm. There were always a few corners in a room where a policeman's vision would be limited at night, and if all the lights were turned off in the villa, it would make the situation even more precarious. The police would be like sitting ducks, while the enemy remained hidden in the dark. This was something in detective work that they tried to avoid at all costs. They could not let sacrifice and loss be the price they paid for breaking a case.

The force had dealt with a case like this in Rezhou before. They could refer to that experience and bring their power into play from many angles. Plus, Rezhou, situated in the southeast along the sea, was home to a very elite unit of a naval special forces team.

When Chen Sheng was in the army, though he had only raised pigs, he had always especially admired that unit. Because of that admiration, after being discharged and returning home, he used his status as a veteran to make a special trip back to their base for a tour. He was extremely impressed with some of their training exercises, several of which involved live ammunition. They didn't fire at moving targets nor fire at long-distance ones. They would instead fire while positioned on a sampan in the waves upon the sea. They would practice firing under unstable conditions like these, where firm decisiveness would be required when pulling the trigger. The second exercise Chen Sheng had witnessed was the long distance running under heavy packs, not on flat surfaces, nor on mountain paths, but on the sandy beach shore or on snow-covered ground. They especially chose the soft beach sand or ground that was thickly covered in snow, for these required great lower back and abdominal strength, as well as great physical coordination. The third training exercise involved the unit dropping out of the sky from a helicopter hovering twenty meters in the air. The cabin door would open and commandos would descend rapidly from it on a secured cable all in the space of three seconds. Their bodies were completely unbalanced in such state, and they had to keep from spinning on the cable and to begin firing as soon as they hit the ground.

This special forces unit also had a special skill in throwing stun grenades that deafened, blinded, and enveloped everything in smoke. A special forces soldier had to have very sharp eyes in a situation like that in order to swiftly occupy an advantageous position. Chen Sheng thought, *The first thing the special investigation team brings in to handle the Carnival case will surely be that team.*

However, in a high-end housing complex like the Carnival, the police were afraid that bringing in a team like that wouldn't work. There was not enough space between the villas to comfortably accommodate a helicopter and furthermore, Zhang Guoliang would by then probably already be ensconced in some corner of the villa. Moreover, it was night. The windows in Building 3 in A Block were all sealed tightly, and the only way in or out would be through the front door. It wasn't like there was any terrain to seize, so using a special forces unit like that would obviously have been a little like 'using a cannon to kill a mosquito'.

The clubhouse to the rear was serenely lit. The rooms in the clubhouse to the rear used for entertaining which faced the outside passageway were lit normally in order to fool Zhang Guoliang. However, the lights in rooms behind these burned brightly indeed. The first was a large room, one originally used for billiards, but was now packed with a squad of riot police carrying loaded firearms. These young warriors usually underwent a lot of daily training, but now that it was time to face a real battle, they couldn't help but become a little nervous. Some were downing water like crazy, while others couldn't keep from vomiting.

This was another team that the police would certainly consider using if they could. Even if that unit was never ultimately used due to restricted conditions and circumstances, they nevertheless had to be there. They were there for their power and prestige, and to maintain public order. You could say that they made for good television, since the whole unit looked pretty darn sharp, they were extremely photogenic.

The news media had already ensconced themselves in a small room in the middle of the house. All were specialists in public security, but the contrast between their image and that of their actual counterparts in the Public Security Bureau was as stark as black and white.

Generally speaking, experts in computers, video, sound and wireless transmissions are a very nondescript bunch of individuals, but once hired by the Public Security Bureau, they became a different kettle of fish altogether. They underwent a subtle transformation and took on a very strict demeanour.

There was also another small room where several leaders were overseeing the operation. Civic leaders, party leaders and bureau leaders were all crowding around a plan of the housing complex that someone had dug up, while they were pointing here and there at it. Their attitudes were like those of self-satisfied generals you might see in the movies. They were the big-shots whose ideas were always the wisest. They might have been arrogant, but they were no-nonsense and pragmatic as well. They would be discussing breaking the front door down and taking Zhang Guoliang by force, discussing waiting for a moment when the suspect's guard was down, then launching a lightning-like, sudden and violent attack. This is when Public Security's 'three-man unit' would automatically come to their minds.

If the three-man unit were to show up, then it would be curtains for Zhang Guoliang. This was what Chen Sheng was worried about. Though physically, Chen Sheng was still far away from the housing complex, the only thing he could think about was what was happening inside. He had constantly been trying to anticipate

Zhang Guoliang's every move, and most of the time he had been guessing right. He knew that Zhang Guoliang would have been precise in all he had done up until then, and would feel himself to be invulnerable from both the front and the rear. But maybe because he had overlooked the child having a phone, or maybe because Long Haisheng might have transmitted a message through some alarm, the terrible consequences of his mistakes were gradually beginning to make themselves felt. *What to do? What to do?* Only then did Chen Sheng really understand the meaning of the Chinese expression, 'The whip won't reach its target' or the meaning of that other expression, 'Water far away cannot extinguish a nearby fire'. No matter how good his plan may have been, it simply could not stand up to the mistakes Zhang Guoliang had accidentally made at the scene.

Chen Sheng had once heard about the three-man unit many years ago. There had been a case that year in Rezhou City where an off-duty policeman was murdered on his way home from work. That policeman was working at the Liming Police Station, but he lived in Sanjiaomenwai, a village to the north. You could reasonably say that nothing was particularly dangerous about the policeman's job since he rode a motorcycle and he carried a gun. However, when he hunched over while riding his motorcycle, the gun on his hip became especially prominent and the concealed weapon became visible. Moreover, the place he rode his motorcycle through to and from work was considered to be Rezhou's 'dark-underbelly', its slums.

There is a saying in Rezhou, 'The coffins are only carried until Sanjiaomenwai'. This meant anytime anyone found themselves in Sanjiaomenwai, things could always easily go south. Funeral processions in the past would always stop at the border of Sanjiaomenwai. When the procession reached this point, the deceased's family would all stop and kowtow to the coffin, then send it on to the graveyard on its own. In other words, Sanjiaomenwai was a slum at the edge of the city, a desolate place, and it was the place where that policeman was targeted.

The motorcycle that policeman rode all the way to and from the bustling Liming Road was impressive in its power and speed, but trouble was waiting for him there when he got to Sanjiaomenwai. In a well-planned attack, criminals intentionally ran a bicycle into his motorcycle, leaving the officer completely smashed and battered, lying flat on his back. The hoodlums who ambushed him swarmed around him, then grabbed that policeman's gun and ruthlessly shot him dead with it. This incident did not garner much attention at first because no one thought that it was premeditated, just some reckless violence that had randomly happened on the street.

However, a similar event occurred again one week later in Sanjiaomenwai. Again, a lone policeman was attacked and shot to death with his own gun, which was then subsequently stolen. This was an organised, deliberate and targeted terrorist action that happened in the very same place as the first. Furthermore, the public all knew now that two guns had fallen into the hands of hoodlums, and no one knew what they would do with them next. There was a period when none of the residents would walk the streets alone or even go outdoors at night. Policemen dared not wear their uniforms, nor would any of the stores stay open after dark.

The Public Security Bureau was not going to take a thing like this lying down. They had a lead which quickly grew legs, for they had an informer who told them that he had seen a deadbeat from the east end of town named Ah Si lurking around Sanjiaomenwai.

The East End was eight or nine kilometres away from Sanjiaomenwai. If you considered how inconvenient the transportation was getting there, and if you considered that Ah Si had no friends or family who lived in the area, for him to suddenly start appearing in that district certainly seemed very fishy. It was a lead worth checking out. Ah Si was selling tea-stained hard-boiled eggs in the doorway of some house in an alleyway in Sanjiaomenwai. Nothing about this fact in itself was suspicious, but it was doubtful, considering Ah Si's abilities, that this was his only way of making a living. *Perhaps hidden in the back of Ah Si's mind, he harboured even greater ambitions?* Then one day, on the pretext of having tea-eggs delivered, the men at the Public Security Bureau invited Ah Si to come inside their offices.

The men at the Public Security Bureau knew a type like Ah Si was generally a troublemaker, so they didn't waste any of their breath, but directly unleashed their wolfhound on him. Ah Si sat in the interrogation chair with both of his hands handcuffed to the chair.

The wolfhound very slowly approached Ah Si, his head held low, pretending not to see him. Suddenly, he stood up on his hind legs, placing his two front paws upon Ah Si's shoulders. Ah Si had once seen something like this happening before, and it was then that he pissed his pants. If this was a trick, it never fazed the wolfhound, who was obsessed with sticking out his tongue and crazily licking Ah Si's face. Ah Si snapped his head back, twisting it back and forth, but he couldn't get the hound to stop licking him, first all over his nose, and then all over his mouth. Ah Si had no idea how long the wolfhound would go on licking him, but what he was afraid of was that the dog was next going to bite and take a piece out of him.

Ah Si begged the Public Security men to save him. He told them he would come clean, that he would spill the beans and give up the names of the people who had snatched the guns. Later, it was said that the 'three-man unit' dispatched by Public Security crept up on a house located in Shiliupu, then while watching each other's backs, and in perfect coordination, one member of the 'three-man unit' banged down the door while another went in firing with the third man right behind him, ready to back him up, and just like that, the fight was over in an instant.

Although this had happened nearly twenty years ago, the coordinated actions of the 'three-man unit' had continued to be a special topic for training inside the Public Security Punishment and Investigation Unit.

The Passing Time Was Torture

Had the 'three-man unit' already been dispatched to the scene at the Carnival housing complex? Chen Sheng didn't know, but from the way it looked to him, they were probably already there.

Perhaps that 'three-man unit' was at that very moment in the room with the leaders, listening attentively to their instructions and analysis in regard to the layout of Building 3 in A Block; discussing the number of hostages inside, how many might be tied-up, how many more might be relatively free, what their present positions might be and the kinds of contingencies they might expect when they broke down the door and stormed inside. They may have been discussing the kinds of lights might be on the ceilings, whether they were fluorescent or incandescent ones, and whether by smashing them they could disrupt the suspect's field of vision.

They were probably also discussing what their own roles would be after they went in, who would fire the first shot, what he would aim at, what problems they could resolve with a second shot, and what they could accomplish within the space of three shots. They would be discussing the risks they faced by going in at night, by fighting in the dark, as well as alternative plans of action. They decided that there would be so many problems inherent in going in at night that the unit couldn't dare risk a night operation.

The three-man unit would by then have retreated to another room to clean their guns while they waited. Even if they were in the habit of often cleaning their guns, in a tense fire-fight, if a gun barrel became burning hot, a bullet could jam inside of it. It was hard to say if a gun would jam, but they felt better off cleaning them anyway. They could always find something to talk about, even though the mood was somewhat oppressive.

One asked, 'How many bullets have you fired?'

The other replied, 'I fired four. I haven't cleaned it since training this afternoon.'

The first one said, 'I originally had a full mag, but this afternoon some brass came down to inspect the shooting range and had me squeeze off a few rounds.'

The last one said, 'My gun misfired during training

this afternoon. I wonder if there are any more duds in my mag. . . ?'

The three later agreed, 'It won't matter, we're good enough that we'll probably just need a single shot. We won't need a second.'

They guns they used were .64's with magazines that held seven bullets. The gun was an older model, but it didn't pack much recoil, so its accuracy at short distances was not bad.

They again put their heads together and talked tactics for a bit. One took the lead and began speaking, drawing out diagrams on a white sheet of paper and going over the procedure they would follow after they broke down the door. The soldier speaking said he would fire a first shot at something that would crash and make a loud sound, like a ceiling lamp, a mirror or a fish tank, before anybody really had any idea of what was happening. The ensuing loud crashing sound would make an ordinary person instinctively want to cover their ears and dive for cover. That would be the moment that second and third shots would go off, and find their target. Of course, if the first shot were to nail the suspect and settle the matter, then that would be all the better.

Danger was definitely closing in on Zhang Guoliang. It seemed imminent. It was palpable. Yet, Zhang Guoliang still hadn't the slightest idea of what was happening. If security at the Carnival housing complex had not been sealed up so tight, Chen Sheng would have certainly stealthily found a way in. He had already thought up a sneaky way of getting himself inside by using the names of several bosses he was acquainted with who were living there. There was Ah Kang, who manufactured eyeglasses, and there was Ah De, who made lighting equipment. There was Ah Guo, who did electroplating, Ah Sheng who made leather shoes, and there was Ah Long who made lighters. The Carnival was a desirable place to live and everyone knew it. For a while, whenever anyone would bring up the name of this housing complex, Chen Sheng would find himself repeating, 'Yes, I know so and so who lives there, and I know so-and-so who lives there, too.' All he had to do was correctly repeat the block and building number and the security guard would let him swagger right into the housing complex. However, whether or not he would be able to get near Building 3 in Block A, it would be difficult to say. What if Chen Sheng were at that very moment to yell, 'Zhang Guoliang! Run! Run quickly!'? The night was so still and everything so quiet that his voice would pierce the air, like glass smashing on the ground, or a dog howling at night in the mountains, and that would be sure to warn Zhang Guoliang.

Zhang Guoliang's nerves would surely be very taut, his consciousness particularly sensitive. Most likely, he would immediately pick up on the slightest abnormal sound or movement outside. It would simplify everything if Chen Sheng were to just yell. All Zhang Guoliang would have to do then would be to obediently come out of the villa with his hands in the air and let the police capture him without a fuss. After he later told them the truth about what really had happened, about all the unsuccessful attempts that Chen Sheng had made to get back his money, would the police still consider him to be the villain? The most they might do would be to tell him that the way he had gone about collecting the debt was all wrong. They might make him undergo some re-education, and they might detain him for several days, but then they would surely let him return home.

But as things stood now, Zhang Guoliang was already trapped like a turtle in a jar, and Chen Sheng was not prepared to risk yelling. He thought, *It would all be ok if I could just call him on his cell.* When it came to Zhang Guoliang's cell, he had deliberately avoided calling it for safety's sake from the very start. When he went to Zhang Guoliang's home to find him, and after he had brought him back to Rezhou, even during that time they were rehearsing their plan, never once had he contacted him by cell. He had done this for Zhang Guoliang's benefit as well; nothing was on his cell, no information, no messages. Then he thought, *How great it would be now if only I had Zhang Guoliang's cell phone number!*

The last time he called Zhang Guoliang's cell phone was many years ago. He wondered, *Did he still even have the same number?* He recalled his number sounding something like the lyrics from a song, or at least that's how he remembered it at the time, that it seemed to flow like water. He could remember the number started with 1340 and that it had ended with 64777, but he had forgotten the digits in between. He wanted to try and dial it, but immediately gave up on that idea, since whether he got through to Zhang Guoliang's cell or not, even if his cell were turned off, or even if that number had been disconnected, as soon as Chen Sheng dialed it, it would leave a trace on his own phone. Later, if the police began to analyse the case, his cover would be blown and all his prior secrecy would have all been for naught.

*

At the time, Zhang Guoliang still felt safe. His feeling of safety came from the fact that he was not being greedy, but merely collecting a debt, and now he was just waiting for the money. All he had to do was wait until tomorrow, and then as soon as the money was in his hands, his task would be fulfilled.

When it came to the measures he took to restrain Long Haisheng's family by tying them up, those were just mere formalities to him, more symbolic than anything else. His objective had never been to harm anyone. Those had just been safety measures. This was why Zhang Guoliang remained calm through that entire night. For everyone's convenience, he had left a small light on in the bathroom, and he also left the air-conditioner on high. Since the family had to sleep on the couch and would not get a good night's sleep, he thought that at least the air-conditioner might make it easier for them to cope. He even untied Long Haisheng's hands from behind his back to make it more comfortable for him to rest, although he still left them tied in the front just like his wife's. It wasn't that Zhang Guoliang wasn't worried, he just didn't anticipate that anything might go wrong or that anything unforeseen might occur. He felt somewhat secure.

Zhang Guoliang thought everyone would probably be able to sleep a bit, even under such restricted conditions. They might not sleep deeply, but perhaps they might at least relax and nap for a bit without a problem. After having gotten to know the family over the course of an evening, he found them to be extremely cooperative. *It was true!* He thought, *This can't be easy on any of them, but at least they understand me now, and that makes it a little easier for everyone*. Throughout the long night, Zhang Guoliang never felt the least bit sleepy. His unfamiliarity with his mission, and the adrenalin rush he was feeling under the circumstances made him very nervous and alert. He still needed to defend himself and he still needed to persevere. The work he still had to do kept rushing through his mind, and this drove him on.

Zhang Guoliang sat down on the recliner without ever relaxing his grip on either the money or the remote control. He didn't need to sleep, for he was used to going without sleep for long periods of time. Before, when he was still living in Rezhou, he would often work through the night if the boss told his workers that they really needed to make a deadline. He could work non-stop both day and night. He had a strong spirit and never knew what it was like to be tired. He always got done what needed to be done. Chen Sheng once told him that money had gone to his head, that it was money that drove him. It was money again that was driving him on this night too, that was his stimulant. Now, Long Haisheng and his family were in front of him, and they were under his control. He told them, 'I'm sorry for putting you through all this. If we can make it till dawn, then all of us will be free.'

They ignored him and were in no mood to contradict him. It seemed like all they wanted was for the time to pass, or perhaps in their hearts, they were hiding an even greater hope. Zhang Guoliang had no way of knowing. They had closed their eyes like they were trying to rest, or were trying to save their strength. Long Haisheng was sitting on a different recliner with his head back. Now that his hands were tied in front of him, he was much more comfortable. His wife and the nanny were scrunched up on the couch so that the child, who was obviously sleeping soundly, could stretch herself out. She lay there, arms and legs splayed, perhaps never being aware, even from the start, that there was any kind of danger. Perhaps in her heart, she knew the whole thing was just a game. Maybe it had something to do with the deliveryman costume Zhang Guoliang was wearing, or maybe with the way he had behaved and acted. Generally speaking, Zhang Guoliang felt that the family had been relatively easy to control. Maybe they had finally realised that they had been the ones in the wrong, especially Long Haisheng. He must have been doing some soul-searching then, or perhaps thinking of the Chinese proverb, 'A single slip brings everlasting sorrow'.

Zhang Guoliang Never Returns, So Someone Has to Collect His Body

Chen Sheng worried all through the night, but now it seemed like the night had flown by. He had stayed holed up at the inn, but found both sitting and lying down to be unbearable. Though he normally never smoked cigarettes, on that night he smoked them until the ashtray was piled high with butts.

When dawn began breaking, Chen Sheng immediately got up and went out again, hailed a cab and headed over to the Carnival housing complex. The Carnival was well known, so most drivers knew its address. On the way over, he explained to the driver that he was actually on his way for some morning exercise, that it was his habit to exercise every morning and that a public park had just been built directly across the Carnival. He heard that it had beautiful scenery, really good paths and no crowds, so he wanted to go have a look. The driver murmured his agreement while zipping along at a good clip in his cab.

The cab traveled east, then stopped directly in front of the Carnival's front gate. After getting out of the cab, Chen Sheng crossed the road directly to the park. He wanted to give the impression he had come there to exercise and that he was itching to get on with it. As he crossed the road, he kept glancing left and right, pretending to watch for oncoming traffic, but was in reality looking over toward the Carnival's front gate to see if he could analyse the situation and determine what might be going on inside.

The police cars were still parked outside, police tape was still hung around the scene of the crime, and auxiliary police in blue uniforms were still standing in a line. The whole scene seemed to be more or less the same as it had been the previous evening. Chen Sheng thought, *There doesn't seem to be much going on inside. Perhaps it's like I imagined, perhaps the police were never really there because of Zhang Guoliang.*

Chen Sheng did not go back inside the little house again. He was right beside it, and it might have made sense for him to go up to that third floor where he could carefully spy on whatever was happening, where he could get a better read on the situation. The water and biscuits Chen Sheng and Zhang Guoliang had left inside would still be there. Perhaps their fingerprints and footprints would still be there too. Chen Sheng thought, *If in the end, the police can't break this case, the house may become a point of interest to some nosey detective. He might make it a part of the case file, and if it stuck in his mind, and if things were to take a new turn several years from now, there might be a treasure trove of evidence left there.*

Still, Chen Sheng felt that he couldn't go back inside the house a second time. Perhaps there was already a police unit waiting in an ambush, or maybe they were watching the house from afar, waiting for a suspect to step inside, then they would sweep him up in their dragnet. He knew he shouldn't even stop for a moment in that area, so he carried on pretending like he couldn't hold back his excitement at the prospect of exercise. Like a bird joyfully flying into the forest, or an animated fish leaping into a river or the sea, he took a deep breath of the park's fresh air, merged with the flow of the other walkers, and then disappeared.

The hills in the park looked as if they had been brought down from outer space, and the trees looked as if they had been pruned and cultivated by supernatural beings. The paths meandered in and out of serene and secluded places, and the stream in the park added music to the air. It was truly a great place for power-walking. Chen Sheng really felt like letting his legs loose and for just a moment to be as free as he liked, but he just wasn't in the mood, he just couldn't make the effort. All he could think about was Zhang Guoliang! If everything was going according to how he imagined, then Zhang Guoliang would only have completed half of his mission. The mission wouldn't be over until all was said and done. If Zhang Guoliang never made it out, then it could never be said that he completed his mission.

Chen Sheng didn't dare go far, but merely meandered around near the vicinity of the Carnival housing complex. He stayed on the grass, or in the pavilions where people were practicing yoga, wielding long tasselled swords, or doing Tai Chi. He watched them absent-mindedly, making sure to keep some space between himself and the Carnival. If the Carnival were now the maelstrom, he wanted to be sure he remained at its edge, yet he still needed to feel its rhythm, keep his finger on its pulse every passing moment in order to feel at ease. Probably an hour had passed when Chen Sheng unintentionally found himself near the exit to the park. He subconsciously cast a glance over at the Carnival opposite, then stared blankly for a moment. *The police cars! The auxiliary police! The police tape! They're all gone! What happened? Had something unexpected happened causing the police to move inside? Had Zhang Guoliang successfully availed himself of their negligence to make a crafty escape? Would Long Haisheng come out now and announce to everyone, 'Everything's fine! We've managed to resolve everything ourselves!' Would it all end on a humorous note like that?* He didn't know. He just didn't know. For some inexplicable reason, Chen Sheng suddenly started feeling nervous and like getting out of there pronto.

Where should I go now? All he could do was go back to the inn. *Was it like I imagined? Had something happened? Had Zhang Guoliang escaped? Had they worked things out?* He felt he had to get back to the inn to wait for any news, otherwise, his heart just couldn't take it.

He tried imagining what might have happened early that morning. Zhang Guoliang would have risen very early that morning and directed the family to go about their business as they waited for whoever was bringing the money, but he couldn't for the life of him imagine what might have happened next. Chen Sheng tried imagining for while, but then finally snapped out of it. He had also tried imagining the ways in which Zhang Guoliang might have escaped from A Block Building 3. He imagined him escaping like in the movie *Escape to Victory*, or like an eagle taking off from a roof, its wings beating so hard that they loosen the clanging tiles. Neither of these scenarios, however, was likely to be happening.

Of course, he found it even harder to imagine Zhang Guoliang dashing along the street with a bag full of cash, not with 300 000 *yuan*, nor even 60 000 *yuan*. He kept on imagining these different scenarios until his mind went blank. Then, another sequence of events, another set of imaginings began creeping into his brain. He imagined a thick and covert police presence, then a scrum of armed riot police, then Zhang Guoliang all bound up in police tape . . .

Chen Sheng was lost in these foolish reveries in his room when he heard a rustling sound coming from beneath his door. He peered out the peephole to see what could be making the noise. It was an attendant stuffing a newspaper under his door, the *Rezhou Informer*. Actually it was more like a circular than a paper, he supposed it had been included in the administration fee that he paid to the inn. *Who would ordinarily read such a newspaper?* he wondered. With nothing else to do, Chen Sheng picked it up and began skimming through it. He hadn't even turned to the second page before he saw an eye-grabbing headline, '*Home Invasion and Robbery at the Carnival.*' The underlying caption read:

Suspect Takes Hostages
Negotiations with Police Going Nowhere

Chen Sheng's head immediately began burning; It looked like things had really gone wrong! But, what nerve did the paper have to write this?! The way they put it sounded problematic, for they had written it as a break in and a robbery, that the culprit was a kidnapper and that police negotiations had gone nowhere! Chen Sheng pored over the rest of the article. It was still ok, pretty much all empty talk, all hearsay, like rumours you might hear on the street, and still not nearly as bad as what he had been imagining. This was yesterday evening's news, news that a daily newspaper would have had to have in before closing deadline, news that a rushed and lazy reporter had essentially scribbled down from a statement some mouthpiece had given that had no real substantial content.

After Chen Sheng had calmed down a little, he thought, *I will wait until the afternoon for the evening edition. The evening edition may report on the results of the police operation.*

Still, thoughts of Zhang Guoliang making a clean escape kept flickering inside of Chen Sheng's brain. *What was a police cordon, what was tight security to Zhang Guoliang?* It may theoretically have been impossible for him to escape, but what if the police had unexpectedly been careless? Then it might have been entirely possible. What if, for instance, while some policeman was rushing around, he slipped and fell into the fishpond? Everyone would be shouting and in the chaos that ensued Zhang Guoliang might have made his escape. When he first arrived at the house, Zhang Guoliang wore deliveryman's clothes. Maybe by then he had thrown one of Long Haisheng's nightgowns over his shoulders, pretended to have gone out making inquiries, then hid in the shadows. Anything was possible, for after all, Zhang Guoliang still had a little of a villager's cunning left in him.

Both morning and noon had passed like this and now it was well into the afternoon. Where could Zhang Guoliang have gone to? If he had a bag of cash in hand, he may have felt it inconvenient walking the streets. Perhaps he was first hiding somewhere, lying low for a little while, for at a time like this, the police would surely be combing the streets. Where could he possibly go? Could he be outside the city under some bridge or in some hole? Or perhaps in the shade of some culvert under a road? Or perhaps he was in the home of someone he was extremely tight with, someone from his hometown, someone who he had never told anyone else about before? With his thinking so scrambled, Chen Sheng welcomed the early arrival of the evening edition.

He bought the paper at the cigarette stand near the entrance to the inn. The first article threw him for a loop. The headline read,

Carnival Robbery Case Broken and
Hostages Rescued, Suspect Shot Dead!

It even had a photo.

As soon as he saw it, he knew it was Zhang Guoliang. His body was lying face up on the couch, his eyes staring blankly at the ceiling, his arms and legs splayed. He was still holding a plastic bag in his hand, the black kind used for household waste. Chen Sheng supposed the money was inside. After he put down the newspaper, Chen Sheng suddenly felt a wave of dizziness and pain in his heart as if it were about to explode. Cold sweat began dripping from the top of his head and his hand that was holding the paper began shaking uncontrollably. Chen Sheng, fearing he was losing his self-control, sought to hurry back to the inn. His room was on the second floor, but when he grabbed the handrail, he discovered he didn't even have the strength to raise his foot to the first step. He thought, *If I were to look in the mirror now, I'd surely see my face has turned ghostly white*! When he had returned to his room, Chen Sheng sat down on the bed stunned, not knowing what to do next. Zhang Guoliang had been the one among all his acquaintances that had been most dear to his heart. He was someone who he had often thought about, and now he was suddenly gone, transformed into smoke and ashes, floating off to who knows where. Chen Sheng knew a catastrophe like this was already far beyond the scope of anything he could possibly deal with. *What shall I do next!?*

How could he have ever imagined that Zhang Guoliang would be shot to death? When they first hatched their plan, it was for them to merely secure a spot of business together. The way they saw it, what they were doing was justifiable, even reasonable. They never even imagined they might possibly fail. They thought that in a place where the economy was so chaotic, that was so rife with gangsterism, that what they were doing was nothing short of ordinary.

Of course, they had also considered what might happen if they could not subdue Long Haisheng. They had talked about what would happen if by chance Long Haisheng overcame him as soon as he opened the door. The most that might happen then would be that he would receive a vicious beating, then be kicked out of the villa or be dragged down to the local police station. At the police station, the police might shackle him and force him to stand in the dreaded Qigong position to try and get him to give up his ringleader or any of his other accomplices one by one. The most the police could really do then would be to tell Zhang Guoliang that the way he had gone about collecting the debt had been wrong. How could they have ever imagined things changing as dramatically as they had, imagined them moving in such a different direction from what they had originally planned? Had they ever once thought that Zhang Guoliang might ever have to pay with his life? If they had, would they then have still taken the risk? This was a possibility that they never discussed.

Chen Sheng had gradually begun to cool down. His previous fantasies about what had happened at the Carnival, about what Zhang Guoliang had been up to and everything else, had all been useless ruminations. When the sky had gradually begun lightening, he had imagined Zhang Guoliang, Long Haisheng and his family awakening. *Oh no! Zhang Guoliang would never have even slept. He would never have been able to. It would've been just like overtime to him. He knew how heavy his responsibilities were, and knew the closer he got to victory, the less he could afford to slack off.*

*

Long Haisheng and his wife seemed then to be napping, or at least they were pretending to be. The nanny and child were both asleep on the large couch, the nanny with her arm around the sleeping child beside her. They were so still, in fact, that they must have both been sleeping, or they would never have been able to stay in the same position for such a long period of time

Just before 6 a.m., it seemed everyone became revitalised, as if they had just made it through a long winter.

The way that everyone began going about their own business made them seem like one big family. As far as Zhang Guoliang could see, the atmosphere then was no different from that of the previous evening, when the last thing they had talked about was raising the money. Now that it was morning, all they had to do was wait patiently. When the doorbell rang and the money had arrived, then everything would be fine; Long Haisheng and his family would be free, and Zhang Guoliang too would have accomplished his mission. This was an outcome everyone was prepared to welcome.

When the child said she wanted to go to school and the nanny told him she would help the child wash up and brush her teeth, Zhang Guoliang never suspected a thing. He was naturally supportive, even to the point of inquiring, 'Shall I first boil up some water for noodles? You'd better at least eat some instant noodles this morning.' He followed the child and nanny with his eyes as they entered the bathroom and then closed the door…

Perhaps this was when the child pulled out the phone she had been hiding and again put it to use, transmitting some crucial message. She could have sent a message to management, to security, to the owners' committee, or even to the retail kiosk at the front gate. It wouldn't have mattered because no matter who she contacted, they would have immediately passed on the message to the Public Security Bureau. Perhaps she sent something like, *We are*

in the bathroom. . . Mother and father are on the couch. . .
The villain seems to be tired. . . His guard is down. . .

No one knows how long afterwards it was, but approximately several minutes later, the doorbell began to ring in Building 3 in A Block. Long Haisheng, as if talking to himself said, 'Maybe the money is here.'

Long Haisheng's wife, with her head tilted to the side, called out, 'Who is it?'

A reply came from the door, 'It's me.'

Long Haisheng asked, 'Is that you Ah Yuan?'

His wife looked over at Zhang Guoliang, as if awaiting instructions. Zhang Guoliang said to her, 'Go and see who it is.'

Perhaps Zhang Guoliang really was tired, for he sat on the couch without ever getting up or taking any kind of safety precautions. Long Haisheng's wife briefly hesitated, then went over to the door. She made a big deal of looking through the peephole, then turned around exclaiming, 'It's Ah Lei!'

Long Haisheng interjected, 'That's my apprentice, the one you heard on the phone last night.'

Zhang Guoliang then nodded slightly to Long Haisheng's wife, who then opened the door. From where Zhang Guoliang was sitting, his view of the door was entirely blocked by Long Haisheng's wife. No matter how he might have craned his neck, there was no way for him to see who was on the other side. Suddenly, as if Long Haisheng and his wife had rehearsed it in the past, the wife first moved sideways while dropping to the floor while Long Haisheng threw himself down on the floor as well.

Zhang Guoliang was still clueless as to what was going on when the three-man unit burst through the door in lockstep and put a bullet through his head. The three-man unit didn't use the .64 this time so as not to disturb the neighbours, and instead used the even higher accuracy Belgian Browning A1910 with a silencer. . .

If Zhang Guoliang had not been killed, but only injured, then perhaps Chen Sheng might have stood up, admitted to being his accomplice, then taken a share of his culpability. Now it was too late for that.

Chen Sheng Vows to Repay Zhang Guoliang No Matter What

The individual key to the entire affair was Long Haisheng. If he wanted to pretend he was innocent, just a victim of circumstance and that it had been merely bad luck that brought the desperate Zhang Guoliang to his door, then there was nothing much anyone else could say. Now that Zhang Guoliang was dead, only Long Haisheng knew the truth, and everything would come down to his version of the events. If Long Haisheng could live with his conscience, not say a word about their secret back-story, then it would remain that way and the matter would be put to rest.

It was all over as far as the Public Security Bureau was concerned. Everything had gone flawlessly, from the time they'd taken on the case, to the time they deployed, from preparation to implementation, from the manpower to the physical resources they used. They had shown such dedication, working night and day to do their utmost to ensure there were zero losses, and in the end the operation had gone off perfectly. Even the dynamite, the deadly weapons and the reported handgun were, after examination, all determined to be fake (the dynamite was made of sausages, the remote control was from a Gree Electric air conditioner and the handgun had been fabricated during the initial report to the police). Still, Public Security had to be prepared for those weapons to be lethal and for the crime scene to be dangerous. They had to assume it was real, just in case. What if the suspect had had been dead set on blowing himself up from the beginning? The destruction would have been incalculable, so they were determined to stop it at any cost.

From an analytical standpoint, there were indeed many doubts that were still left surrounding the case. First of all, Zhang Guoliang was from out of the area. He carried with him no ID, and there were no messages left on his phone. It was clear that he had gone there prepared and that he had not arbitrarily chosen that particular home.

Second, where had he gotten the deliveryman costume? How had he slipped so easily into the Carnival? How had he known about A Block Building 3? Clearly, he had come prepared; was there someone else behind the scenes as well, someone who instigated him to commit this crime?

Third, how had the family been able to report the crime to the police from inside the townhome? The atmosphere must have been fairly relaxed inside.

Fourth, and key, what had Zhang Guoliang gone there to do? If he had gone there to collect payment on a debt, then why hadn't Long Haisheng mentioned it? If he had gone there to rob them, then why hadn't he absconded as soon as he had hold of the money?

Fifth, he had stayed there the entire night, how had he gotten along so well with the family that whole time? Why had he stayed there so long? There had been no signs of any struggle and no one had been harmed in any way. It even seemed like he had allowed the family to get on about their daily business.Unless they had a Sherlock Holmes in the Public Security Bureau – someone who might've felt there were still a few fishy details left over about the case, who might've enjoyed mulling them over, analysing and deducing facts, ferreting out people's motives and establishing parameters and possibilities in the case – then it seemed that these possibilities would just have to wait until another day.

Chen Sheng didn't know how he would ever checkout of the inn, how he would ever return home, or how he would ever return to his store. He could tell everyone that he had been taking care of business for the past few days, making a loop around Jiangsu, Zhejiang and Shanghai, but then realised that he just couldn't be bothered. He wasn't too anxious to go home to his wife and children again either. The only thing in his head was Zhang Guoliang, his voice and features, his smiling face, the way that he looked a little like a black bear.

It was only several days earlier that this simple and honest man from the countryside had left his home in Le'an to follow him, his heart filled with a vision for the future, happy at the prospect of doing a little business, but because his own miscalculation, and because of a mishap, Zhang Guoliang was now shot dead. Cheng Sheng felt so sad, that it was like his entire body had been steeped in some kind of medicine, some chemical. He was totally oblivious as to what to do next.

After coming to a little, he realised there actually were a few things that needed doing. He needed to go see Zhang Guoliang! Where was Zhang Guoliang now? Where could he be? He would, of course, be lying on some cold slab in the mortuary.

Cheng Sheng had a friend at the mortuary who he asked directly if the police had set up any surveillance where he worked. Chen Sheng explained how he knew Zhang Guoliang, but of course, never let on about their present relationship. His friend understood and arranged to take him there to see the body after he got off work. Chen Sheng had been upstairs in the funeral parlour before during the times when he sent off a few old friends. However, this was the first time he had been to the morgue, which was downstairs. They went down a gloomy corridor, which looked as if it had just been washed down, and there were gurneys lined up on each side. There was a red light slowly turning up ahead, as if showing the way. It somehow created a very depressing atmosphere.

Chen Sheng asked his friend in a low voice, 'What's with the red light?'

His friend replied, 'Nothing. It's just a reminder to people, so they don't give rise to any illusions while they're down here.'

It dawned on Chen Sheng, *If it weren't for the slowly turning red light, that place would indeed have seemed just like hell!* They arrived at the morgue, and Zhang Guoliang was lying inside. There were several refrigerators for individual bodies on one side of the morgue. His friend told him that rich people would rent these since they were a little cleaner, and that Zhang Guoliang was most likely in the general storage. The morgue's general storage looked like a freight container. This was 'steerage'. When his friend opened the steel door, a blast of cold air streamed out.

Zhang Guoliang, labelled a 'John Doe', had been put together with victims of traffic accidents, as well as those who died from suicide, either drowning or jumping. They were all, regardless of sex or age, kept inside this storage container for a specified time, until it was determined that no one was coming to claim them. After that, they were taken out and cremated.

Chen Sheng watched from a distance as a mist enshrouded Zhang Guoliang. His deliveryman clothes were now frozen and looked like plastic. His limbs, probably frozen in rigour mortis since the time of his death, looked extremely awkward. His face was covered in frost, like he had white whiskers growing all over it. The bullet hole in his forehead had already scabbed over, making it look like a very large mole, or like a birth-mark. He no longer even looked human. Chen Sheng started to retch, but then covered his mouth to try and keep himself from vomiting. This was a physiological reaction, but even more a psychological one. The two of them had originally been in this together. Now, one of them was still breathing, while the other was lying in a morgue. The contradiction was just too great. Later, after returning upstairs, Chen Sheng vomited several times. Upon returning home, he couldn't stop vomiting until his face was filled with snot and tears.

His wife asked him, 'What's wrong with you? What's gotten hold of you?'

He told her, 'It's nothing. You wouldn't understand even if I told you.'

Chen Sheng would often think of Zhang Guoliang lying in the morgue, and sometimes while engaging in self-reflection, he realised that he too had become frozen. He had become as hard as steel, and he felt he would remain frozen for a long time to come. Never again would he be able to return to his family, and the fact that they did not yet have any inkling of this was terrifying to him. *No, I cannot leave things undone like this*! Although he couldn't do anything openly for Zhang Guoliang, he could not simply leave him lying there.

He thought of a civil case, one that had happened many years ago in Rezhou, back when he did business in the industrial zone. At a factory's construction site, a worker from the countryside had been crushed to death by a bulldozer. The driver absconded, and the ID he left behind was fake. The bulldozer had no registration, for it had been purchased after being written off for scrap, and its registration was fraudulent. The factory boss had no choice but to report the incident, so he went to the local police station where they told him there that they only dealt with public security matters, and that the accident was an internal company matter. The boss then reported it to the traffic police, where they told him that although the man had been crushed to death by a vehicle, it had not happened on the city streets. Alas, all the factory boss could do was to have the body refrigerated, for the worker could not be cremated until the affair had been cleared up. Yet, he couldn't afford to *not* have him cremated, for the costs of keeping him refrigerated were increasing day by day.

Later, after more than ten days had passed, the deceased's father rushed over from Qiangling in Guizhou, while his wife, pregnant with the deceased's child, rushed over from Shijie in Dongguan, with others having to pay for her trip. The thing was, they couldn't afford either, the refrigeration cost or the cost of the cremation, let alone pay for their trip back home with his ashes. Chen Sheng recalled in the newspaper report about that case, something the deceased's father said had made his skin crawl. The old man said, 'I have no money. Either I leave him here, or I go sell a kidney, then come back and have him cremated.' Later, some public judicial Assistance Centre appeared to help sponsor the cremation costs and get the family back home.

Why not have a look and see if I can find that Assistance Centre? Chen Sheng snapped out of his reveries a little and then he had this thought, *Whatever else happens, this is the least I can do for Zhang Guoliang! It would be better than doing nothing, and after doing it, I might just feel a little better about myself!* When someone dies, it is sad, but if they become a lonely soul, a wild ghost after death, then that is truly a tragedy. It is said when a corpse is recovered, it must be recovered whole. Although Zhang Guoliang's corpse was a little worse for the wear and tear, still, it was fundamentally whole. But, if no one were to come claim him and bring him home, then this would be even more tragic than if his body had been mangled.

But where was this Assistance Centre located? Was it a non-governmental agency? Or, was it a service entity belonging to the Ministry of Justice? The key thing was, what would he tell them about this matter? Would he have to provide details? Could he be vague? If he was forced to let the cat out of the bag, then not only would searching for it not help Zhang Guoliang, but he himself might be dragged into it too!

Chen Sheng tried searching on the internet, and sure enough, he found a website called the *Rezhou City Judicial Assistance Centre*. It seemed to be bona fide. The website had several photos of the Centre's inaugural meeting, and they were recruiting volunteers who wanted to enter community service. Their ranks were huge, with more than ten branches, their strength extended through the city and even out to the country-side. It listed an overview of their services as well. *What was this entry*, Empty Nest Seniors Fighting for Their Rights and Benefits? *What was this post*, Standing Up Bravely for the Truth While Demanding the Return of Justice *and so forth. . .* ?

Chen Sheng thought, *What would be a good cause for Zhang Guoliang*? Maybe something like, *Help the*

Deceased to Peacefully Return Home! or *Give the Family Sponsorship*!

Any ordinary person might see any of these causes to be justifiably righteous, but to Chen Sheng, there was no more righteous cause on earth than his own. Zhang Guoliang had died because of him, and he was going to think of every conceivable way he could to help Zhang Guoliang's family members to be able to make the trip to Rezhou.

Without further hesitation, Chen Sheng left this message on the Assistance Centre's platform:

It seems very likely that the man who died at the Carnival housing complex was Zhang Guoliang. He had previously come to Rezhou for work. I believe he was from Le' an in Jiang Xi. You should help him by finding his family for him. After all, he was human too.
Watertight

For the next few days, Chen Sheng didn't have much appetite, and he never did go to his store. He remained on the Centre's website day and night, and left other messages on the Centre's web page as well:

He is so pitiful. Could it be that his family still

doesn't know? It is truly sad. Might someone give him a little help? I myself would pay if I could.

And in a different tone, he wrote:

He is dead and gone! Perhaps he never really wanted to live. There are too many people like him these days. His crime still lingers, even after his death.

Someone else with doubts about the case had also left a post. They were either some kind of expert analyst, or perhaps just some busybody with too much time on their hands, but Cheng Sheng was stung by the relevance of what they said:

Maybe the person who keeps leaving these messages is the instigator. Otherwise, Zhang Guoliang would've never known where to go by himself. Perhaps he'd been working behind the scenes, perhaps he never went himself because he's too selfish. It's the same as if he had committed negligent homicide himself, or as if he had watched someone else die, yet never went to save them.

Another is dead, yet he still goes on living. How does he live with himself? He should apologise by taking his own life, by dying himself!

This shook Chen Sheng. It suddenly seemed like he was being spied on, like someone knew he was hiding behind the scenes. He stared obsessively at his computer screen without moving. Chen Sheng now also began thinking about how sarcastic those messages were.

Hmph! One can't take talk on the internet like this seriously. People love heckling others on the net. These things they're saying, all of it is just cheap talk. Still, Chen Sheng also had to admit that the things they were saying were true and that they really hit home.

It's true! Zhang Guoliang was dead and he himself went on living, but how was he to ever find peace? *If I keep thinking about Zhang Guoliang every day, is this peace? If I even dream at night that I've become Zhang Guoliang, is this peace? I once even cried out 'Dada!' for some inexplicable reason. Someone from Rezhou would never call their father 'Dada'! It's almost as if I am possessed! Anyway, when it comes to that talk on the net, why should I ever 'apologise by taking my own life'? Why should I die? What would my dying now ever prove? Would my death bring Zhang Guoliang back to life? If I were to die now, wouldn't it just be like I was cutting off my nose to spite my own face?* Of course, when he thought about it, just going to the morgue or trying to help Zhang Guoliang's family by looking on the internet wouldn't be enough. He had to do more, or it would simply become too difficult for him to go on living. He simply couldn't take it. He might go on living, but he wouldn't be more than the walking dead. He was so tormented, so tortured.

Chen Sheng Decides to
Return to Jiangxi

While Chen Sheng was busy with his torment and struggle, the volunteers from the Assistance Centre had already set out on the road. They had likely seen Chen Sheng's messages right from the start, for there was never a moment when there was no one from the Centre online.

They too left messages on the site, inquiring:

Who is this? How do you know all this? Is there anything else you would like to add? How can we get in touch with you? Do you know how we can go about locating his family?

Yet, there was no way that Chen Sheng could reply. He wanted them to think that he was just a good

Samaritan who was merely providing these clues out of the goodness of his heart and that he had no real personal interest in the matter. He wanted to seem as if it didn't really matter to him whether the Centre succeeded or not.

Ever since he had brought Zhang Guoliang back to Rezhou, he'd remained invisible, behind the scenes, and he'd remained hidden for so long by then that he wanted to keep it that way.

The first thing the volunteers receiving his messages did was open an inquiry. They wanted to find the person leaving the messages, but they hit a brick wall. On the other hand, they did find the identity of that person named Zhang Guoliang that Chen Sheng had provided them with as soon as they began searching. There was someone by this name who really did exist. Although there was no name for him in the case file, maybe just 'the villain' or 'John Doe' or whatever, but in the labor market, in the shoe materials market, in the industrial zone, there was indeed a person with such a name, a person of flesh and blood. There really had been a person with that name who had once come to Rezhou to work. They didn't know for certain whether or not Zhang Guoliang was even his real name, since people from the countryside were so adept at using fake names and forged identities. Was this the name that he used in his hometown? Would they be able to find his real family?

However, they surmised that it probably was his real name, since a person from the countryside would not be likely to come up with a name quite like that. To fake a name like that would require some creativity, but in a place where they were so poor that they didn't even have enough to eat, a place so poor that they prayed for salvation from above, a person from a place like that was just liable to have such a straight-laced name like Zhang Guoliang. It only seemed logical to the volunteers.

Now that they had a clue about where to go, they went about things wholeheartedly. The volunteers were young, and young people never think too much before diving into things. But, would they really be able to find Zhang Guoliang's home?

When Chen Sheng had gone to Zhang Guoliang's home to proposition him, he took a very arduous route. This hinged on his reasoning at the time. He didn't need to use his ID to buy a ticket for the train and he had ridden the rest of the way by hitching rides on ore trucks. *Oh! I had almost forgotten! I hadn't made it to Zhang Guoliang's hometown even then, I still had some way to go after that!* He still had to ride the local buses running in every direction, the ones with handwritten signs indicating their destinations taped to their windscreens. On one of them was written, The Old Route.

The Old Route he had taken was an antiquated road that seemed almost abandoned. It was a dirt road, pitch black with no lighting, and it stopped at many rustic villages along the way. The good thing about it was that the route was completely unmonitored.

Chen Sheng had been covering his tracks at the time, and that's why he chose that Old Route. The volunteers, however, would never choose such an exhausting route. They would first take a plane, then drive on a freshly paved road, maybe not a highway, but one that saved time nonetheless. It would be a road that would be a pleasure to drive on, that ran through tunnels in the mountains, thereby straightening out roads that used to be as windy as mosquito coils. It would turn a trip that used to take a full day into a half day affair.

Everything had gone exactly like Chen Sheng had imagined. The volunteers found Zhang Guoliang's home and his elderly father. Just how they went about breaking the news to the old man, Chen Sheng didn't know, but they probably told it pretty much like it was, since the capability of village people to adapt to disaster goes far beyond anyone's imagination. In any case, Zhang Guoliang's elderly father ended up going to Rezhou.

The news of the Assistance Centre's good deeds spread and reporters were soon writing about how they had helped his elderly father to identify his son's corpse, and how they had helped him handle the funeral arrangements. Especially because Zhang Guoliang had been shot to death, his body needed to be made up. The makeup didn't necessarily need be all that great, but the old man at least had to be able to recognise his own son.

The clothes Zhang Guoliang wore at the funeral were not his own, and though they looked somewhat foolish, when they pushed him through the crematorium's doors at that last moment, it was upon a bed of satin that the volunteers had built for him, to keep him warm in the winter and cool in the summer, for only satin was capable of both.

Right up until his death, Zhang Guoliang had never lingered for very long in his hometown. *Give him a cardboard coffin too*! Everyone always needs somewhere to return to, and the cardboard coffin would become a lodge for his spirit, for only then would he really find some peace.

The volunteers even collected donations for the old man. There were not necessarily a lot of them, but enough to make their kindly intentions felt for the time being.

The reporters at times could also be really thoughtless, ignoring everything else in pursuit of their own ends. When the Rezhou Informer published the aforementioned article, it may have overstepped its bounds, for when it came to its gist, it would have been better off entitled something like, *Zhang Guoliang's Elderly Father Extends his Apologies to the People of Rezhou, or He Sincerely Asks Everyone to Forget What Happened.*

They even printed a photo along with the article, a photo of the old man holding a picture of his son prior to his death. The old man had a confused look in his eyes, his face had a stupefied expression, his suffering made explicit by the downturned corners of his mouth.

Had those reporters ever once thought of how that old man might have been feeling when they took that picture, when they were snapping their camera shutters closed???

Though merely a photo, it still spoke of life and death, of *yin* and *yang*, of things that remained the same and of things that changed, of eternal separation. It was the same in spirit as that photo they had taken on the day Zhang Guoliang died as well. It was like the photo of him lying sprawled out on his back upon the couch, his mouth wide open, his eyes in a blank stare and his limbs all askew.

Didn't those reporters ever have any sense of how terrible it was to see Zhang Guoliang like that? It was the same today. Didn't they ever suspect that the old man might already be in enough pain? It didn't do any good! It didn't help! It was no good, it didn't help, why would they take such a photo of Zhang Guoliang's father? Why would they write such things?

This made Chen Sheng even more resolved to do what he had decided to do next. What had he resolved to do? He would now diligently go about collecting debts people owed to him, starting with the most easily collectible debts first. Then, he would earnestly go about liquidating his entire inventory and try to sell the most easily saleable goods as fast he could. He would also put up signs that said, 'For Lease' and 'Favorable Terms' on his store. He had done this many years ago when he was fighting to survive in business. Now, whoever wanted could take away everything at a discount.

His wife grilled him, 'Chen Sheng! What's the matter with you? Ever since you came back from your last so-called 'business trip', you simply haven't been the same!"

Chen Sheng didn't bother to explain, but told her instead, 'I'm through with the business. The business is killing me and I want to wrap it up quickly.'

His wife told him, 'You're crazy! If you don't do business, then what will we eat or drink?

Chen Sheng told her, 'If you love eating and drinking so much, then you can't count on me anymore!'

Chen Sheng had become resigned by then, and his mind had become as clear as a bell. *If I can't handle even this one thing well, then what's the point of me going on living? How can I ever keep my business? How can I ever keep on making a living? I will never be able to do it!*

The only people Chen Sheng couldn't forget about were his parents. When he went to see them, the time they spent together was hellish! He'd paced back and forth before them, not knowing what he should tell them. His father and mother were both very proper. One had been a government official, while the other had been a retired head nurse, so he knew that for them to have to hear a story like his would be unbearable for them. Yet, he couldn't bear not telling them. There were two reasons why.

First, he had been the one involved in the Carnival case. He had recruited a man, but due to his carelessness and an accident, he had gotten that man killed. His parents were mortified upon hearing what had happened. His father took it the hardest. It had seemed as if he were about to collapse, as if his soul had suddenly been sucked right out of him. Chen Sheng thought he might suddenly be having a stroke, and so he asked him, 'Is your head pounding? Are you able to roll your eyes?', but it turned out that he was ok.

The second reason he gave them was this, 'Although I'm very sorry now, I was the cause of Zhang Guoliang's death! I now need to protect Zhang Guoliang's elderly father, to observe Zhang Guoliang's filial duty in his stead. I need to go stay in Le'an in Jiangxi, perhaps for a very long period of time. The two of you can forgive me, but there is no way that I can ever ask Zhang Guoliang for his forgiveness. I'm now living in his shadow, and this is the only thing that I can do.'

His mother was not totally opposed to his decision, but only said, 'You give it some more thought. Isn't there any way that we can compensate them with money instead?'

She added, 'For you to have to go live in a farming village in order to care for his father just doesn't seem fair!'

Chen Sheng told her, 'It is fair. Had Zhang Guoliang even ended up a cripple or as an invalid, at least then his father would still have a son.'

His mother didn't respond.

*

Chen Sheng asked Zhang Guoliang's elderly father what route he would take home, then he secretly accompanied him the entire way back. While first riding the train, then while taking the bus, he watched him attentively from a distance as he cautiously escorted him home. Zhang Guoliang's body had by now been moved from the morgue into a small box. His elderly father held that box in his hands, never putting it down for a moment. He sat like a statue throughout the entire journey; never moving, never eating or drinking. He wore only two expressions the whole way; either sitting stupefied looking out the window, or furtively wiping away his tears from his eyes. Chen Sheng followed Zhang Guoliang's father all the way back to Le'an. After returning, the old man did not come out of the house for three whole days. Those were the three days in which Chen Sheng waited for him by his door.

On the fourth day, his elderly father finally opened the door and came out. When Chen Sheng went to greet him, he almost didn't recognise him. Over the past three days, Zhang Guoliang's elderly father would've spoken to his son of many things, spoken of family affairs, of their relationship as father and son, of where they were going to go from there. He would have spoken to him until his mouth had gone raw, until it was full of blisters. Looking ahead, there were going to be even more changes than there had been before.

Chen Sheng told him he had come from Rezhou and that he was thinking of staying on so he could be near him, so he could help him to get along.

The old man asked him, 'Are you a volunteer? If so, there's no need for that! I'll be fine on my own now.'

Chen Sheng then took out a shoebox and opened it. In the box there was 300 000 *yuan*. This was the money he had managed to put together by liquidating his business. It was everything his family had at that moment. He had been thinking about the many excuses he would give the father to explain where that 300 000 *yuan* had come from. He wanted to tell him that he and Zhang Guoliang had earned the money together, that they had partnered together in a bit of business and that they had a verbal agreement about what would happen if things went well, or what would happen if he were locked up for three to five years, how that money would be Zhang Guoliang's...The old man never even gave Chen Sheng a chance to open his mouth. Zhang Guoliang's father interjected first, telling Chen Sheng how the volunteers had already done so much for him, telling him that it was already enough. He said he only spent a single *yuan* every time he ate, and that with the money they'd given him, he could eat for an entire lifetime and never run out of money.

Maybe the old man really and truly was grateful to those volunteers, or maybe he wanted to intentionally avoid anything that reminded him of Zhang Guoliang's trip to Rezhou. Yet, the more he continued refusing the money, the more Chen Sheng couldn't stand it. He got down to his knees before him imploring him, 'It was I who made Zhang Guoliang go to Rezhou! It was I who put him in a situation that he couldn't get out of. . .'

As the old man looked at Chen Sheng, he began clutching at his clothes, as if trying to prevent himself from fainting. His mouth trembled violently, but not a single word came out of it. Perhaps over the past few days, he had already said all he wanted to say to his son and now there was nothing thing left to say. Then, he hauled off and punched Chen Sheng with what was more like a muffled slap . . .

After he had been slapped, Chen Sheng felt a bit better. It meant that the old man still needed someone he could vent to, it meant that he was right to try and protect him. He couldn't just pay lip service to protecting him, he had to make it real. Chen Sheng realised then that he had to find a way to make a living there! *Maybe I can do a little business here. There aren't any Long Haishengs here and maybe the environment for doing business is a little better.* People from Rezhou had the special trait of remaining undaunted by repeated setbacks and of really being able to spot an opportunity.

What business might possibly do well in Le'an? Chen Sheng remembered hearing people say that there were lots of abandoned uranium mines in the area. *Why not find someone to help me contract one out with, then sell the uranium we mine to the Iraqis?*

Chen Sheng then remembered that they were fixing the roads in Le'an. He had seen the men working on them before. The workers had thickly calloused hands, and during the winter, they used coal to keep themselves warm. *Maybe I could supply them directly with coal, or maybe even open a supply warehouse for the workers?*

Later, after Chen Sheng had some time to mull it over, he thought, *Maybe opening a small supermarket would be best! People from Rezhou opened supermarkets everywhere, and wherever they opened one, there was always a queue out the door. We know how to supply goods and we know what people need. Opening a supermarket here in Zhang Guoliang's hometown would probably be the most practical thing I could do.*

When he had the time, Chen Sheng could also go over to Zhang Guoliang's mushroom shed, to the place where he first found him when he came to Le'an. He could also go by the family house as well, maybe sit for a spell on some mornings. He'd been the one who had taken Zhang Guoliang away from this place. He thought, *If I do well and make a good showing, then Zhang Guoliang's old man might eventually come around to accept me!*

A month later, Chen Sheng's mother called to tell him his father had died. Chen Sheng hastened home to bury his father, but his heart was conflicted, for he knew that if he had never done what he had, then his father never would have died so young. His father had been a cautious man throughout his entire life. He was such a sensitive soul that a thing like that must have scared him half to death. Chen Sheng told his mother to take care of herself, to keep on keeping on, that although he was in Le'an taking care of Zhang Guoliang's father, he could immediately return to care for her if ever she needed him to.

Another month passed before his wife's lawyer arrived in Le'an to find and serve him with papers outlining her three reasons for wanting a divorce. The reasons were:

First, Chen Sheng had a bent personality that precluded him ever succeeding in business, and that she had always resented him for this. Second, his enlisting of Zhang Guoliang to collect a debt meant he himself was a fool. Third, his return to Le'an because of this affair showed that he had long ago lost his mind.

His wife said the scheme seemed harebrained from the start, that all signs indicated that it was, and that Zhang Guoliang was merely some acquaintance, it was not like he was ever Chen Sheng's partner or anything, he was just someone he happened to know. If she had to live with someone like Cheng Sheng any longer, she wondered, how exactly would she ever survive?

Chen Sheng had nothing more to say, so he signed his name on the divorce agreement. He also agreed one by one to all her other conditions. He thought, *My wife is right, I started all this. I'm the one who was wrong, so it's only fair that I should walk away from our marriage empty-handed . . .*

A Story of Friendship and Trauma by Chi Zijian

Ji Lianna passionately tends to her flower garden and avoids looking back at her life with remorse. Xiao'e does not know the first thing about plants and cannot stop thinking about her past. Eighty-year-old Ji Lianna is a child of the Jewish diaspora, and young Xiao'e is not sure whether she is human at all. The two women could not be more different. Yet, in a numbingly cold Harbin flat in an old Russian villa, an unlikely friendship blossoms between them. Soon their dark histories come back to haunt them as they realise they have more in common than just a shared address.

Translated from the Chinese by Poppy Toland